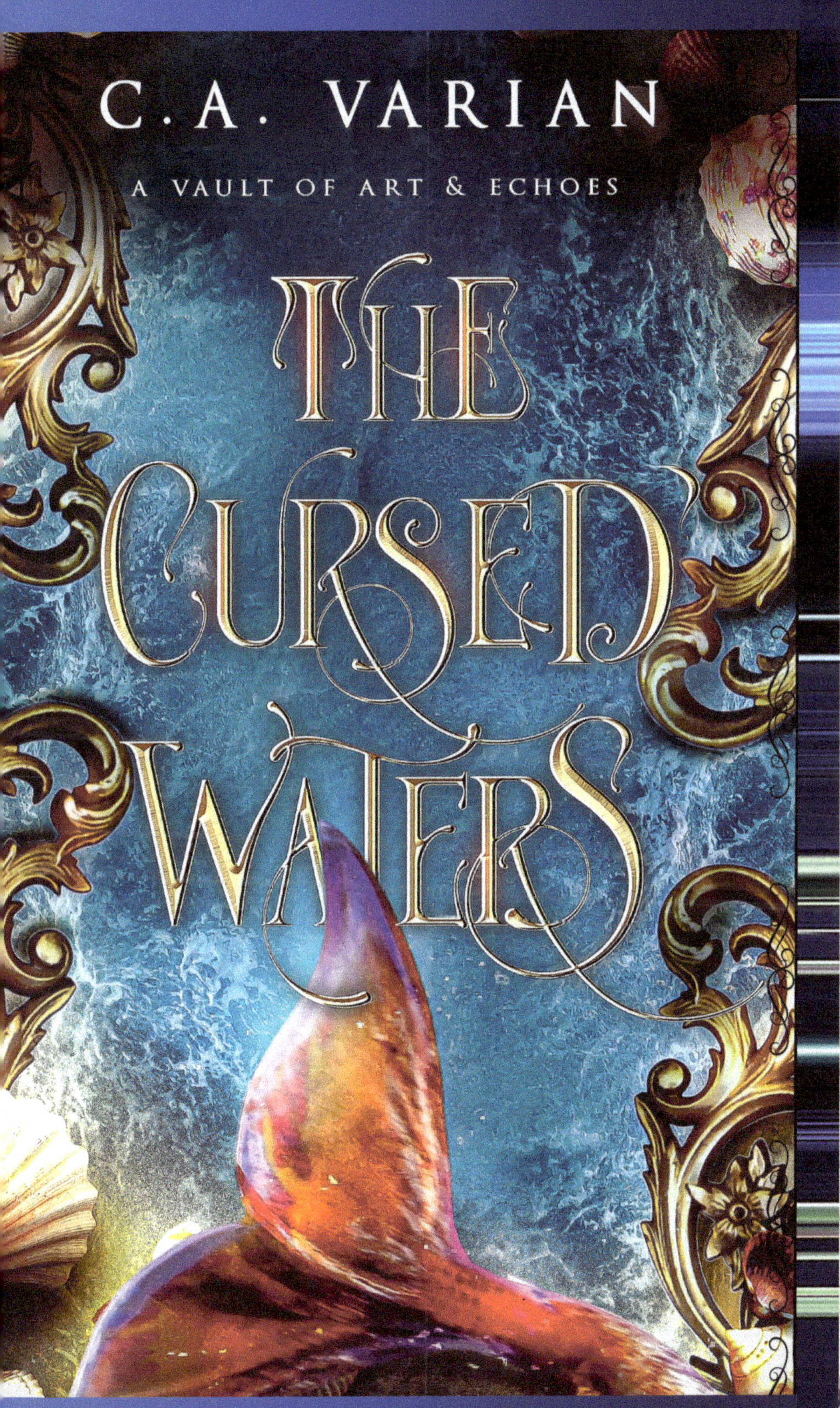
C. A. VARIAN
A VAULT OF ART & ECHOES
THE CURSED WATERS

Main Book Cover by Graphics by Geka ISBN 9781961238657

Hardcase Design by D'Arte Oriel

Alternative Cover Design by D'Arte Oriel ISBN 9781961238701 Paperback 9781961238695

Edge Design Artwork by D'Arte Oriel

Edge Design Embedding by Painted Wings Publishing

Title Page Design by Lucenthaven Covers

Scene Break Design by Anastasy Helter

Activity Pages Designs by J. Paige (My amazing assistant, Jessica!)

Full Artist & Designer Credits in Back of Book

First edition 2025

Main Cover Hardback ISBN 978-1-961238-65-7

Alternative Cover Hardback ISBN 978-1-961238-70-1

Alternative Cover Paperback ISBN 978-1-961238-69-5

Thank you to my talented and hardworking Executive Assistant, J. Paige! I don't know what I would do without you...probably curl up in the corner of a dark room...if I'm being honest.
XOXO,
Cherie

Born of Broken Chains

With my mind and body still reeling from what I'd done, the endless ocean folded around me, its colors shifting like bruised glass. Light moved through the water in slow ribbons, never quite reaching the ruins below. There was no surface here, no sky. Only the breathless weight of the deep, and the quiet that followed after something terrible had been undone.

Miris was gone.

The throne she once ruled from still waited. It remained unchanged in form, but it was no longer hers. Carved from coral and power, it rose from the reef as it always had, unshaken in form and unmistakable in presence. But the weight it once held had shifted. No queen ruled the sea now. Not yet. Not until I took my place.

And beneath me, the water stirred with quiet urgency, answering something it had already accepted. It coiled around my arms and shoulders, drawn to me with a cautious sort of pull, as though trying to understand who—or *what*—I had become. It didn't shrink away. It didn't lash out. It simply moved, and I moved with it, suspended in the space between what was and what might be.

This place still carried her imprint. The scars would take time to fade, but the current had already changed. It no longer dragged. It no longer burned.

The magic that lingered here was ancient, older than language, and it pressed against my skin with the same heaviness I felt in my chest. Not pain. Not quite power. Something between the two. The kind of pressure that makes you aware of your own heartbeat.

I didn't know what kind of queen I would become. I only knew I wasn't her.

And that, for now, was enough.

Markos drifted to my side, his presence quiet but steady, a warmth threading through the cold press of the deep. He didn't speak. He didn't need to. Just being near him calmed the storm that had been rattling through my chest, steadying me in a way words never could.

When I turned to him, the look in his eyes undid me more than any crown ever could. He didn't see a goddess. He saw me, exactly as I was, and he stayed.

The silence between us wasn't empty. It was full of everything we'd endured to reach this moment, everything we hadn't yet spoken aloud. I let it stretch for a few heartbeats, then finally said, "I never wanted this."

"I know." His hand found mine, fingers lacing through with unbreakable support. "That's why you'll be different."

His touch was firm, not possessive. A grounding weight in a world that still felt like it might dissolve beneath me. The ocean curled around us with expectant magic, the kind that didn't demand—it waited. Behind me, the throne loomed in the shadows. Not just a seat, but a relic of a past carved by fear.

I glanced at it, then back to Markos. "What if I fail them?"

"You won't." His thumb brushed over my knuckles. "But even if you did, you'd fail as yourself. Not as a monster in someone else's shape."

I almost smiled at that. *Almost.*

In the distance, the merfolk remained still. Watching. Hoping. Some of their faces were unreadable. Others looked as if they didn't quite believe they were free. And maybe they weren't—*not yet.*

Freedom, after all, wasn't something you were given. You had to learn to carry it.

"I don't know how to begin," I said quietly, almost to myself.

"You already have." His voice was soft, but it landed like truth.

Standing there for a moment longer, I let the tide move around us. I thought of everything I'd lost. Everything I still held. I thought of the pain, and the love that had endured it. Then I drew a breath and let it go slowly, releasing the fear that clung like seaweed to my ribs.

I didn't let go of his hand, but I did start forward.

The throne waited at the reef's edge, shaped from stone and shell and slick with age. Its surface held the pale polish of salt, but the power it once commanded still pulsed beneath the quiet. It didn't rise in glory or collapse in defeat.

It endured.

Every part of it carried her presence. Miris had ruled from that seat with a heart too hardened to hear anyone but herself. She didn't guide. She commanded. Those who knelt before her weren't subjects. They were prisoners waiting for punishment. This wasn't a place where decisions had been weighed with care. It was a place where power had been spent without mercy.

I drifted forward, and the water seemed to thicken with every stroke. I could still feel what it had meant to kneel before that stone. The sting of defeat, the bite of helplessness, the slow unraveling of hope... those things had happened here, and the sea hadn't forgotten.

Reaching the base of the throne, I let my hand find the edge of the coral. It didn't recoil. The surface felt smooth beneath my fingers, shaped by generations of tides, as if the ocean had been trying to wear down what she built long before I ever arrived. I held that thought for a moment—what it meant that even the sea had grown tired of her reign.

Still, I didn't sit.

Instead, I looked beyond it. Merfolk watched from the shadows, some with guarded faces, others with something closer to hope. None of them moved. They didn't bow. They didn't speak. They simply waited.

Blowing out a breath, I let my palm fall away from the stone and turned to face them fully. I had once stood here in chains.

Now I stood as myself.

SIREN SECRETS

"Explore the sensation of transformation—
from human to mermaid, from innocence
to desire, from solitude to obsession.
What does it feel like to change?"

Describe the sensation of your body changing—
scales appearing, gills forming, desire blooming. Is
it painful or exhilarating? Do you embrace your
new form, or do you mourn what you've lost?

REFLECTION

Have you ever felt
yourself shifting into a
new version of
yourself?

What moment in your
life made you feel the
most powerful?

Is transformation
something you
embrace or resist?

D'ARTE ORIEL BOOK COVER DESIGN

D'Arte Oriel: High-Quality Book Cover Designs & More

At D'Arte Oriel, we specialize in crafting stunning book covers that capture the essence of your story. Our services include e-book and print cover designs, NSFW and Non-NSFW illustrations, and much more.

ILLUSTRATED BOOK COVERS:

CHARACTER ART

D'ARTE ORIEL
ILLUSTRATED CHARACTER ART

D'ARTE ORIEL
ILLUSTRATED CHARACTER ART

D'ARTE ORIEL
ILLUSTRATED CHARACTER ART

INTERIOR ART DESIGNS & NSFW:

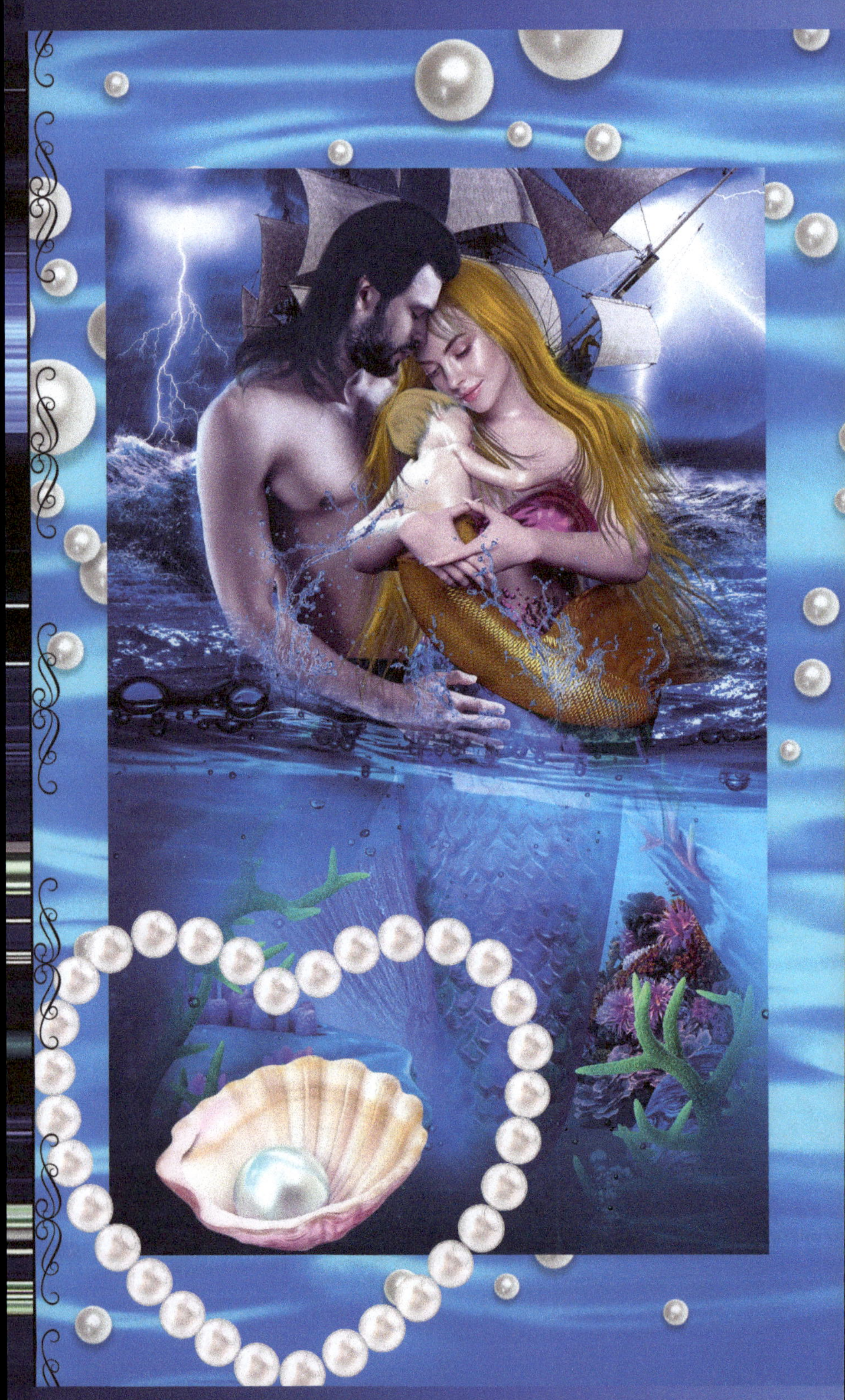

she was made of
STORMS AND
LULLABIES

THE MERMAID'S EMBRACE

BENEATH THE WAVES. WHERE SHADOWS CREEP.
A VOICE CALLS OUT FROM WATERS DEEP.
HER SONG. A THREAD OF SILK AND PAIN.
DRAWS YOU NEAR THROUGH SALT AND RAIN.

OH. SAILOR. LOST UPON THE TIDE.
COME CLOSER NOW: THERE'S NAUGHT TO HIDE.
THE SEA IS VAST. BUT I AM NEAR:
LET GO OF FEAR. LET GO OF FEAR.

HER EYES. A STORM: HER TOUCH. A FLAME.
SHE WHISPERS SOFTLY AND SPEAKS YOUR NAME.
IN HER EMBRACE. THE WORLD WILL FADE.
A LOVE ETERNAL. COLDLY MADE.

OH. SAILOR. DROWN WITHIN MY LORE:
THE SEA SHALL CLAIM YOU EVERMORE.
NO LAND TO TREAD. NO SKY ABOVE.
ONLY THE DEPTHS AND ONLY MY LOVE.

C.A. VARIAN
THE CURSED WATERS DUET

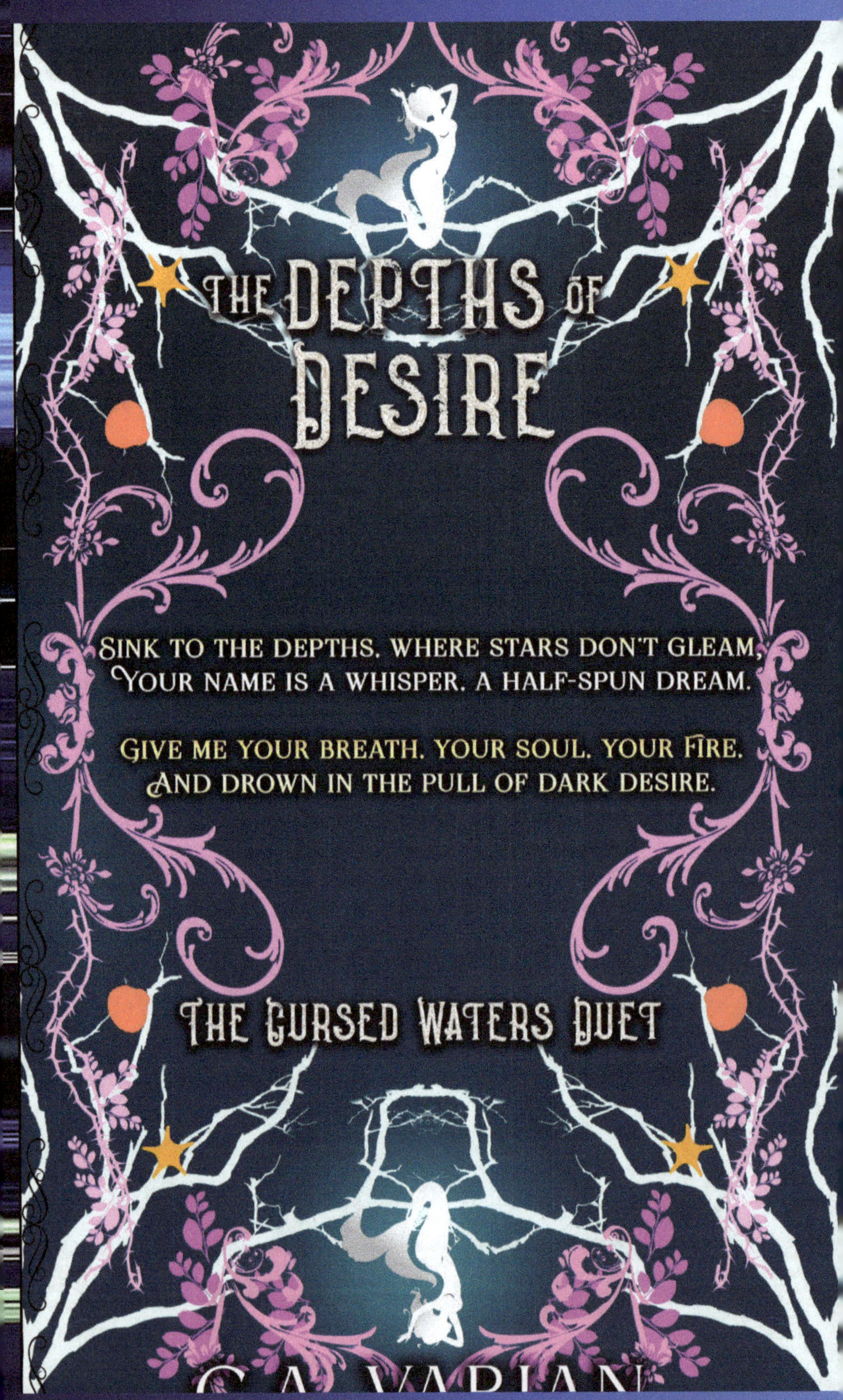

THE DEPTHS of DESIRE

SINK TO THE DEPTHS, WHERE STARS DON'T GLEAM,
YOUR NAME IS A WHISPER, A HALF-SPUN DREAM.

GIVE ME YOUR BREATH, YOUR SOUL, YOUR FIRE,
AND DROWN IN THE PULL OF DARK DESIRE.

THE CURSED WATERS DUET

C.A. VARIAN

Character Word Search

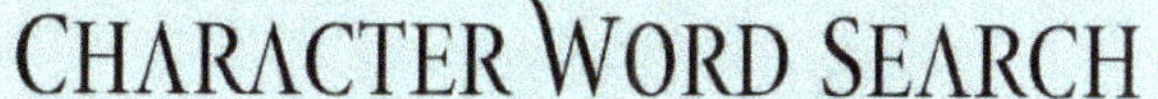

```
L M K F D C S U J K C G F N M
X U V I L G K Y S O J E P E S
J T R O Y J A P V C T O N S H
P P O A Z U R E X E C R Q T T
P E K I P L P J G V O G W O I
Z L P M C H L I G I R I P R A
A I C J A S K D Z A I O E A R
D O I E O J L E D A L S B S W
W S D A U V C T Z N E H Y P A
L R O A F S W M C O I O Z A E
A I A I C U L A A O A O X M S
P R Z O E G M A R K O S I X L
Y B R I E O N V V R K R A U N
N D Z D W F I G Y H I G A F H
E I V N S H H U X S L P O M G
```

AZURE	GEORGIOS	MIRIS	OONA
CORILEIA	LUCIA	NESTORAS	PHAEDRA
ELIOS	MARKOS	OCEVIA	SEAWRAITHS

Frina Art

The Crown Beneath the Waves

MIRIS

They buried me in silence.

No songs. No salt-blessed rites. Only the sea, cold and indifferent, pressing me into the dark like an afterthought. I remember the way the light dissolved above me, each ripple swallowed until there was nothing left but blackness so absolute it felt like it lived behind my eyes.

I had once ruled coral palaces and danced through the warm slipstreams of mermaid courts. My voice could shape tides. My tail shimmered like liquid silver beneath the moon. I was not a goddess, not yet, but I had power enough that others bowed their heads when I passed. Power enough that she, the one who called herself divine, began to watch me too closely.

She was ancient. Sharp-eyed. Her crown was carved from drowned bone and pearls polished by the tongues of the dead. To be noticed by her was not a blessing. It was a sentence. She saw ambition in me and decided it looked too much like her own reflection.

So, she cut it out.

They dragged me in chains to the edge of the trench. Her voice was quiet when she cursed me, almost tender. She called it necessary. Said it was mercy, sparing me from what I would become. Then she tore the song from my throat and sealed my magic beneath my skin, where it curled and festered.

When they cast me down, I did not scream. I had already lost the part of myself that could.

At first, I fought the weight. Marked the time with scratches on stone, counting days in clawed lines that blurred in the current.

But the sea is patient. It stretches time until it loses meaning. Until you forget whether you're still alive or simply moving out of habit.

The cold settled in, not the kind that stings the skin but the kind that dulls it—sinking slow and heavy until I couldn't tell where I ended and the trench began. Thoughts drifted. Memory frayed. My name slipped from me. What remained was bone and breath and the faintest echo of will.

And still, I lingered.

Something in me refused to die. A sliver of self buried too deep to reach. It didn't scream or rage. It waited.

That's when I felt it.

The water shifted, soft at first, brushing my skin like a question. It wasn't the current. It was something deeper—older—threading through the dark like a living pulse. A hum wound low into the seabed. It wrapped around my ribs and settled into the place where my voice had once lived.

I lifted my head for the first time in what may have been centuries, and the trench answered.

The voice didn't speak like a language. It moved through the sea in vibrations, in ancient pressure, in a rhythm that bypassed hearing and curled directly into my spine. I couldn't name the shape of it, only feel its intent. It knew me. Not the surface I'd worn or the title I'd once carried, but the raw wound I had become.

The stone beneath me cracked with a slow, deliberate groan, splitting open as a thin vein of blue light bled through. It flickered at first, a faint shimmer that wavered like it hadn't yet decided to stay, then began to pulse—each beat growing stronger, steadier, more rhythmic, like something alive and waking beneath the surface.

I moved toward it on hands scraped raw, the glow pulling me forward with quiet insistence.

Shell fragments lay scattered across the exposed hollow, tangled with shards of bone and threads of brittle magic. Though thinned by time, the power still lingered—dense with sorrow, heavy with memory.

These weren't just offerings.

They were remains. Evidence of others who had reached this place before me and never found their way back.

The light spilled outward into a circle etched into the seafloor, rimmed with symbols I didn't recognize but somehow understood. A throne without a crown. A wound waiting to be filled. The silence pressed around me as the sea asked its question.

What will you give?

I didn't hesitate because I feared the price. I hesitated because I already knew it. There was nothing left to bargain with. My voice was gone. My power, locked beneath layers of rot and ruin. All I had was what I had become—grief sharpened into purpose.

I pressed my palm into the center of the circle.

Pain bled through me like light penetrating deep water. It didn't slice. It consumed, moving through my veins with slow, searing intent. My skin lit from within. Symbols carved themselves across my arms and into my chest, burning their shape into muscle and marrow. I arched back, but there was nowhere to flee. The sea held me still while the power made room for itself inside me.

Memories that weren't mine flooded in—visions of thrones rising and falling, temples swallowed whole, goddesses turned to bone beneath shifting tides. I saw her again, the one who cursed me. And behind her, others—older, crueler, forgotten by time but not by the sea.

I wasn't the first to be cast down.

But I was the only one still standing.

The voice pressed close again, sinking into the center of me with a clarity that left no room for doubt.

Rise, daughter of the drowned. You are no longer forsaken. You are the deep that swallows. You are the tide that claims. You are the memory the sea does not forgive.

The current stilled around me as the trench held its breath, but then, I stood.

What had once been bone and breath was now something else entirely—stitched with power, wrapped in silence, forged in the weight of every goddess who had dared claim the sea before me.

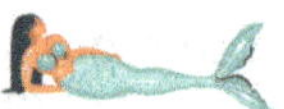

Higher still, the water warmed. Lightened. I breached the shelf and hovered just beneath the pale shimmer of moon-light. And there it was—carved into the reef like a monument to her arrogance: the palace.

It rose just as I remembered.

Obsidian columns stretched from the coral bed, each one engraved with binding runes meant to bend the tides to her will. Statues flanked the entrance, their faces identical to hers—unchanged, unaged. Her worship had endured. The sea still tried to sing her name.

But I could feel the emptiness in those songs now. The depth no longer listened with the same loyalty.

She had let me slip from memory.

Not from cruelty. Not even fear. Something colder. She had deemed me unworthy of attention—discarded like a cracked pearl, cast into the dark with all the others who had dared defy her.

That was her mistake.

I had no desire to crash through her gates like vengeance incarnate. The trench had burned that kind of fury out of me long ago. What stirred now was heavier. Quieter. A stillness that bent the current with its weight. The kind that builds before the sea breaks wide.

She wouldn't see me coming.

For hours, I hovered there in the dark, watching the moon rise higher—its silver sheen stretching in ribbons across the reef. A tide shifted somewhere beneath my awareness. Small. Subtle.

But it answered me.

The sea was no longer hers.

And I had returned to claim it.

The palace waited.

It always had, looming like a scar carved into the reef, monolithic and unmoved by time or current. But as I neared its shadowed halls, the water changed. The current faltered, thickening with recognition. The sea knew what I had become. It knew why I had returned, because it had sent me here.

The temple walls beside the palace were slick with age, carved from obsidian veined with pale coral. Statues flanked the entrance, each still bearing her face—tall, composed, eyes cast skyward as if she alone could command the tides. Once, I might have bowed to that image. Not *now*.

She stood at the altar, her back to me, poised and serene as if this day were just another rite. Coils of pale gold hair trailed down her spine, catching the light like strands of moonlight. Her tail shimmered with pearlescent blue, flawless and luminous. Every part of her was polished, ceremonial, sculpted for reverence, but there was no breath in her beauty. Only the cold gleam of something preserved.

She turned when she sensed me, a gradual motion edged with hesitation, like her body knew what her mind refused to accept. For a moment, she didn't speak. Her gaze moved over me as if trying to see through a fog that refused to lift. She blinked once. Then again. Recognition arrived late, and far too slowly.

I was not the girl she had cast down. Trench light shimmered across my skin. My hair, black as ink, drifted behind me like smoke. My tail no longer glittered with the luster of youth; it thrummed with silver power, pulsing steady and unstoppable, like the current that answered to no one. There was nothing soft left in me.

Her lips parted, her stance going rigid. "You should not be here."

"I never left." The words didn't come from my throat. They moved through the water itself, shaped by a voice older than hers.

She flinched yet raised her hand to summon a spell. Old magic coiled around her wrist like ribbon, reaching for the current, but the sea didn't come. It hesitated, then fell quiet. Her power had faded, while mine had taken its place.

Behind her, the sacred flames at the altar sputtered, then died. Cracks split down the statues' faces, carved by a power that no longer belonged to her.

"You stole from me," she said, her voice fraying like torn cloth.

"No," I said, drifting forward. "The sea simply realized there was someone stronger."

Before I could blink, she lunged, but the water answered me faster. A wave surged from the altar and hurled her backward with the force of an ancient tide. She struck the stone floor, her tail curling in reflex, scales flashing like brittle glass.

I approached slowly, watching the fear gather behind her eyes. It wasn't pain that shook her.

It was understanding.

"You taught me silence," I said. "Now I'll teach you what it means to be forgotten."

She reached for her crown—a delicate circlet of coral and ivory—but it slipped from her fingers and clattered across the stone. I let it fall. I had no need for a crown shaped by her hands.

At the center of the altar, I pressed my palm to the stone. It responded instantly. Light surged beneath the surface, carving itself into new forms, rewriting the temple's name. A pulse echoed outward like a second heartbeat—deeper than sound, older than time.

The sea shifted. The tides obeyed. The statues that remained turned their fractured faces toward me, and somewhere in the dark, the trench exhaled.

I didn't sing. I didn't kneel. I didn't ask.

The ocean had already chosen.

SIREN SECRETS

"Every night, you feel ghostly hands trailing along your skin. Are they a memory, a dream, or something real?"

One night, the hands become solid.
Who do they belong to, and what do they want?

SIREN SECRETS

"Write about a love so deep the sea itself grows envious. What happens when the water tries to take back what it believes is its own?"

Imagine being in love with someone, but every time you're together, something goes wrong— storms rage, waves rise, the sea threatens to swallow them. Do you fight to keep them, or let them go before the ocean claims them?

REFLECTION

Have you ever felt like love was a battle against fate?

What do you fear losing when you love deeply?

Have you ever felt like something outside of your control was trying to take happiness away?

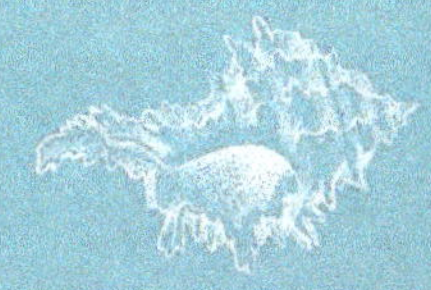

Hello, my name is Keni Aryani aka Babelast.
I am an illustrator with over 10 years of experience working with authors.
I work from scratch.
Customizable and reviseable (only during sketch phase), because I love to capture the feel of the author's story.
I can work in various genres; fantasy, romance, horror, mechanical robots, sci-fi, anything but gore.
This is all the arts I worked for Cherie, she is lovely person and I can't get enough thank her for the chance to introduce myself here.
If you need artist to capture your scene I would love to work with you, please contact me here :

.https://www.facebook.com/keni.babelast/

https://www.instagram.com/babelast.id?igsh=N2R1aDZpdXJ2eGYx&utm_source=qr

Hi there everyone! This is Cangxxx Graphics || Book Designs who loves creating arts since 2016 and always had this dream of seeing our designs displayed on shelves in bookstores and libraries.

CXG specializes manipulated and illustrated book covers specially romance and fantasy. However, we are still flexible with other genres and graphics, and we ensure every artwork that we made is visually captivating, eye-catching and a reader magnet. We are excited to work with more outstanding authors in the future, if you're interested in us send us a message in CANGXXXGRAPHICSOFFICIAL@GMAIL.COM and let's make the best book cover for your books!

REJECTED
DEMON
A DEMON ASSASSINS STORY
AC WILDS

CLAWED HEARTS BOOK ONE
THE LUNAR
LOVE
MATCH
HELEEN DAVIES

USA TODAY BESTSELLING AUTHOR
CURSING
CUPID
HARPER A. BROOKS

A DYSTOPIAN MONSTER ROMANCE
UNDER HIS
VICIOUS
TOUCH
USA TODAY BESTSELLING AUTHOR
ZELDA KNIGHT

CARRION
AS
USUAL
DAYNA HART

AUTHOR NAME
BEYOND
MAGIC

THE COMPLETE HEXALOGY
EVER
AFTERS
ALEXIS VORPAHL

CONSUMED
BY
TEMPTATIONS
KIRA STANLEY

SABRINA
ROZNOWSKI
FINDING
THE
LOST
KINGDOM

E.M. WHITTAKER
VAMPIRIC
SONATA

SIREN SECRETS

"You dream of a presence in the deep—
a figure watching, waiting. Who are they,
and why do they want you?"

Describe the moment you finally come face-to-
face with what's been waiting for you beneath the
waves. Is it a lover, a monster, or both?

REFLECTION

Have you ever felt like
something—or
someone—was meant
for you, even if you
couldn't see them?

Do you fear the
unknown, or do you
crave it?

What do you imagine
waits for you in the
deep, dark parts of
yourself?

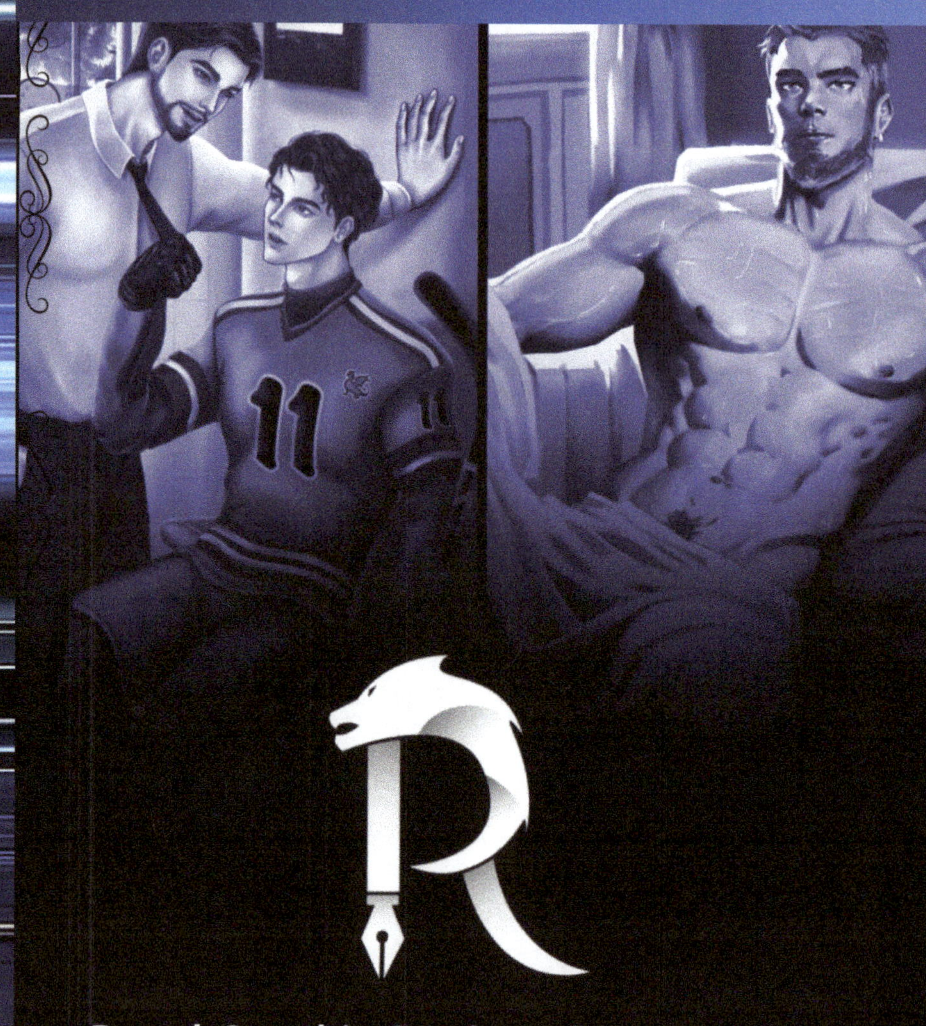

Rosel Graphic Designs is a creative team from the Philippines specializing in stunning book covers, interior designs, character art, and 3D dolls. Whether it's photo manipulation, illustration, NSFW artwork, or motion graphics, they bring ideas to life. Get in touch for top-tier designs at the best rates!

SIREN SECRETS

"The only thing that soothes him is your voice.
When you stop singing, the nightmares return.
Does he love you, or does he need you?"

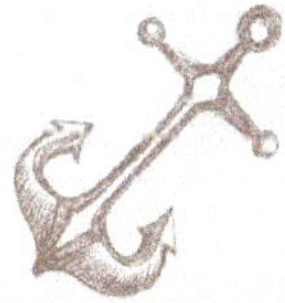

Describe the first night you stay silent.
What happens when he wakes?

Before the Shell

OCEVIA

Eleven-Years-Old

The house was too quiet.

Wind slipped through the garden in uneasy shifts—gentle one moment, sharp the next—carrying a kind of hesitation, like it didn't know whether it belonged. I stood barefoot at the edge of the tall grass, breath coming too fast, my chest rising and falling in uneven rhythm. My hair stuck to my cheeks and my clothes were filthy. I should've been tired after running back from town, but I wasn't. I was angry.

It had started that morning, when I crept behind the velvet curtain outside my mother's sitting room. I'd meant to scare her, maybe make her laugh, but then I heard her voice, hushed and coiled with tension, never meant for my ears.

"It's happening," she said. "Too soon."

A stranger replied in a voice that scraped like driftwood. I couldn't see her, but I smelled brine and burning herbs.

"Have you told her?"

My mother's silence answered first. When she did respond, she didn't sound like my mother at all. The words were too cold. "There's no point. She won't understand. She's already…"

I waited for the rest, but it didn't come.

My heart had beat so loudly behind that curtain, I thought it might give me away, but they never saw me.

I stayed there long after they left, too cold to move, too raw to breathe, every part of me simmering with a heat I didn't understand. When I did leave, I'd ran straight to town. There was nothing there I needed or wanted to do. I just needed to get away.

By the time I returned, the mysterious visitor was gone, but something was moving inside me.

Wrong, something inside me screamed.

A cold, spreading feeling too big to name, pressed at my ribs like it was looking for a way out.

It had been following me for weeks, curling beneath my skin whenever no one was watching. I didn't know where it came from or what it wanted. Only that it was getting louder.

Behind me, the manor loomed. Its silence pressed through the stone like breath held too long. I didn't have to look up to know they were watching from the windows. I could feel it in the stillness. The way I'd always felt their whispers crawling along my spine.

Something's wrong with her. She's not like Elaria. She's not like any child I've ever seen.

I pressed a hand to my chest. My heart was pounding too hard, too deep, like it was broken... like it didn't belong to me at all. The ache spread into my ribs. A hum stirred beneath my skin, building into a thin, piercing note that threaded through my ears like the atmosphere was tearing at the seams.

Everything tilted.

One moment I was standing—wind in my hair, grass warm beneath my feet. The next, the world shifted. I dropped hard to my knees, palms slapping wet ground. Tremors ran through my fingers. Sweat, or maybe tears, clung to my cheeks, and a slow trickle of blood slipped from my nose, wet against my upper lip.

I wasn't sure what hurt.

Only that something had cracked open.

The garden was gone.

Where once had been hedges and flowerbeds, there was only ruin. The cliff side had split wide, its edge fractured and crumbling into the sea below. Trees leaned away from the damage, their branches stripped bare, as if something had reached in and torn the breath from them. The air stung with brine and smoke—a scorched, coastal scent that didn't belong here. It smelled like the sea had come too close and brought something furious with it.

Footsteps crashed behind me. My father's voice. My mother's. But it was Elaria who cut through them all.

"Ocevia!"

From the direction of the manor, she was running toward me, arms stretched wide, but our mother caught her mid-stride and pulled her back. I turned, blinking through the haze, every part of me shaking. All I wanted was for someone—*anyone*—to come close. To kneel beside me. To ask if I was hurt.

But no one moved.

They just stared.

Their eyes were too wide. Their mouths parted but silent, as if frozen mid-word. And in that stillness, my stomach twisted. They weren't going to hold me. They weren't going to reach out.

They were afraid.

I didn't know what I'd done. I didn't even know how it had happened. But something inside me had slipped loose, and whatever it was, they had seen it.

They didn't say the word aloud. They didn't have to.

It settled between us like a weight—quiet in its arrival, heavy in its meaning, final in the way it changed everything.

Monster.

And I understood.

In our house, monsters didn't get to stay.

No one spoke to me after it happened—not for hours, not until long after the sun had vanished behind the cliffs. The manor stayed unnaturally quiet, as if the silence itself might be holding the walls together. Someone left dinner outside my door, but I didn't touch it.

I heard Elaria crying in the next room, her sobs muffled by the wall between us. They hadn't let her sleep beside me that night, and I didn't know why. Only that it felt like something had been taken.

I didn't lie down. *Couldn't.* The air in the house felt brittle, like glass stretched too thin, and I was afraid that if I moved too loudly, everything would break.

Instead, I crept into the hallway and sat outside the study. The stone was cold through my nightdress, but I didn't move. A narrow line of moonlight spilled beneath the door, cutting across the marble like a blade I didn't dare cross. Behind it, their voices murmured low.

"She didn't mean to," my father said, his words slow, heavy, as if each one had to fight its way out. "You saw her face. She was terrified."

"She should be," my mother answered. Her voice was quiet, but it snapped through the silence like a whip.

"She's just a child."

"She's something else now."

I bit the inside of my cheek hard enough to taste copper. My heartbeat had slowed. I was not calm, but still, like animals when they know they're being watched, when they know they're prey. If I adjusted myself even slightly, they'd know I was there.

"She's not the first," my mother continued, her voice softening into something more distant. "Do you remember the stories? My grandmother—the one they locked away before she ever had the chance to shift. My mother swore it ended with her. That it was gone from the bloodline."

He didn't answer.

"She told me it skipped generations. That it only shows up when the blood is stirred. That it couldn't happen again." A pause. "But it has."

"She cracked the cliffs," she continued. "With nothing but her emotions. You saw the wave, Leonas. That wasn't the sea. That was *her*."

Curling my toes into the hem of my dress, I pulled my knees tighter to my chest. I didn't know what she meant. I didn't understand how my worry, or my sadness, could tear the earth or raise the tide. I only knew it had happened.

And it had come from me.

"She's a danger," my mother said. "Maybe not yet. But soon. If we ignore this—if we wait too long—it won't just be us at risk. Other people could get hurt."

A long silence followed. Then the scrape of a chair leg against marble.

"She doesn't know yet," she added. "But she will."

Footsteps approached and then the doorknob creaked.

I barely had time to run, vanishing into the dark just before the door swung open.

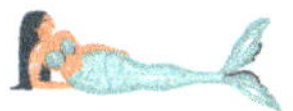

They told me we were going for a walk.

Just a short one, they said. A stretch of air along the cliffs before the stars came out. Quiet. Simple. I didn't ask why. I'd already learned not to. Questions only made my mother sigh. They made my father go still, and I hated that stillness more than I hated her frowns.

So, I nodded and slipped into my softest dress, the pale one I wore on temple days, and followed them through the front doors and down the winding path to the sea.

Elaria wasn't with us.

That should've told me something, but I didn't want to think about it.

The path was lined with dry grass and loose stones that scraped beneath our shoes. My father kept glancing at the horizon, as though something might rise from the water if he stared long enough. My mother's hand stayed wrapped around mine, her grip too tight to be comforting. The smile never left her face, but it looked stretched thin, a shape she no longer knew how to wear.

I tried to mimic it, thinking maybe it would help, but it sat wrong on my face, and the moment I stopped thinking about it, it vanished.

We didn't talk as we walked. The only sounds were the crunch of our steps and the wind weaving through the reeds, sharp with salt and heavy with something unspoken. Each gust pressed a warning against my skin I didn't know how to interpret.

When the cliffs gave way to sand, the air thickened around us, weighted with a quiet that didn't feel natural, as if the shoreline had emptied itself in preparation. The beach ahead was too clean. No footprints marked the surface. No leftover candles from fishermen. No distant songs from the village.

Curling my fingers into the folds of my dress, I looked up at my parents, but neither of them met my gaze.

The wind shifted. It was no longer just sharp with salt but edged with a pressure that made the inside of my chest pull tight. The waves slowed as they reached the shore, each one retreating with unnatural care, as if the ocean was drawing a line. My skin crawled. My ribs felt too small. The air changed.

And the sea lifted her.

A woman emerged from the sea—not swimming, but rising, as though summoned from below. Her silver tail shimmered as it split into legs, moonlight trailing the curve of her skin. She stepped onto the shore without hesitation. The tide drew back from her feet, retreating with quiet obedience, leaving her path dry and unbroken.

No water clung to her. No stumble broke her pace. She moved like the beach had always belonged to her.

Her eyes found mine at once.

Not my mother's. Not my father's.

Mine.

Blood turned to ice beneath her gaze. I took a step back, reaching blindly for my mother's hand, only to feel her fingers clamp around my wrist, not in comfort, but restraint.

"This is her?" the woman asked. Her voice was smooth, nearly gentle, but there was something underneath it, thin and sharp as a filament, threading against the edges of my thoughts.

My father gave a stiff nod. "She's... she's begun to change. The bloodline is strong. Too strong."

Steps measured, she circled me slowly, her expression distant. She didn't look at me like a person. Her eyes passed over me with the detachment of someone reviewing a choice already made.

"She's young," she murmured, not to anyone in particular. "Good. They break more cleanly that way."

Although everything in me wanted to run, my legs refused to move. Every part of me had gone rigid and wrong, like I'd stepped into a current I couldn't fight. My breath came shallow and sharp. My feet felt bolted to the earth.

"Will she remember?" my mother asked, and I didn't miss how her voice cracked when she said it.

The woman stepped in closer and her silver eyes fixed on mine. She held my gaze longer than I could stand, but there was no emotion in their depths, and she answered without blinking.

"She'll remember enough."

A gust pulled at the hem of my dress, seeming to answer for me.

Looking up one last time, I searched their faces for a flicker of softness as my heart wrenched in two, the kind they used to give me when I cried in the night, but my mother turned her face away. My father stared at the sea like I was already gone. A tightness locked across my chest, the sensation creeping in like crushing pressure deep behind my ribs, too sharp to breathe through and too sudden to stop.

That was when I understood.

They hadn't brought me here to help me.

They were giving me away.

IZAAC
BRITO

Hey there! I'm Wallflower Designs, your go-to for all things creative, especially if you're an indie author or a romance writer looking to spice things up! I specialize in custom, hand-drawn artwork that brings your ideas to life—whether it's unique covers, eye-catching logos, or complete branding packages. I also love creating adorable chibis, stunning portraits, and character art that truly capture your vision. If you're ready to book a project or have any questions, shoot me an email at wallflowerdesigns.custom@gmail.com or join my Facebook group, Wallflower Designs. Can't wait to get started!

wallflowerdesigns.custom@gmail.com
Fb Group: Wallflower Designs

wallflowerdesigns.custom@gmail.com

Wallflower Designs
ILLUSTRATIONS & GRAPHIC DESIGN

Wallflower Designs
ILLUSTRATIONS & GRAPHIC DESIGN

BUTTERFLY'S
PROMISE
AUTHOR NAME

HEART OF THE
EVERWOOD
AUTHOR NAME

Wild
FLOWER
AUTHOR NAME

REJECTED
ROGUE
DECLAN RAYNE

DARKEST
BLOOM
AUTHOR NAME

WHITE
SHAMAN
AUTHOR NAME

HI! I am Chan Art.

I've been editing for almost 3 years for international authors.

I offer lots of services like:

BOOKCOVERS

Character Art

Spread

Paperback

Hardback

Header and Breaker

I specialized in making Manipulation and I can't do illustration or drawing.

SIREN SECRETS

Imagine pulling a man from the wreckage of a storm, his body trembling as he whispers your name. How does he know you?
What force brought him to you?
Do you welcome him, or do you fear him?

BOUND BY THE TIDE

A Dark Mermaid Romance Mad Lib

*Instructions: Fill in the blanks first—don't peek ahead!
Then read the story aloud and let the curse consume you.*

Fill in the blanks:

1. ___________________
Adjective (sensual)

2. ___________________
Body part

3. ___________________
Verb (past tense)

4. ___________________
Adjective (forbidden)

5. ___________________
Body part

6. ___________________
Body part

7. ___________________
Sensation (e.g. "pulsing")

8. ___________________
Adjective

9. ___________________
Verb (intimate, past tense)

10. ___________________
Noun (nautical)

11. ___________________
Sound (pleasurable)

12. ___________________
Adjective (sinful)

13. ___________________
Verb (teasing or seductive)

14. ___________________
Adjective (dangerous or dark)

15. ___________________
Body part (intimate

16. ___________________
Emotion (overwhelming)

17. ___________________
Verb (passion, past tense)

18. ___________________
Adjective (possessive)

19. ___________________
Noun (cursed or enchanted)

20. ___________________
Exclamation (gasp-worthy)

She had once been human. (1)_______________, soft,
untouched by the sea's cruel grasp—until the witch took everything.

The curse had stolen her breath, her heartbeat, her soul.
Now, she was something else. A creature of the deep, driven by hunger.

Her (2)_______________ gleamed under the moon as she surfaced,
locking onto the shipwrecked man clinging to the waves. The pull
of the curse (3)_______________ inside her, demanding she take him.

He was perfect. Mortal. (4)_______________ in his terror, his
(5)_______________ trembling as he gasped for air. She reached
out, letting the tip of her (6)_______________ graze his skin,
reveling in the (7)_______________ tension between them.

"You shouldn't have come here," she murmured, her voice
(8)_______________ as the tide. "You should have drowned."

His lips parted, but before he could speak, she
(9)_______________ against him, the wreckage of his
(10)_______________ forgotten as the ocean rocked them together.

A (11)_______________ escaped him as she kissed him—deep,
(12)_______________, claiming. Her fingers trailed over his throat.
His pulse thundered beneath her touch.

"Beg me," she whispered.

He (13)_______________ her name, his body surrendering to her.
He was lost now—just like all the others.

She pressed her (14)_______________ lips to his
(15)_______________, letting his (16)_______________ seep
into her. He tasted like salt and surrender. He was hers.

She (17)_______________ him, feeling the curse
(18)_______________ in her veins as the sea tightened its grip.
The (19)_______________ sealed their fate.

"(20)_______________," he gasped.

And she pulled him under.

CROWNED IN SHADOWS
AUTHOR NAME
REIGN OF THE TWIN DRAGONS
AUTHOR NAME
AUTHOR NAME
ECLIPSE BORN
FROST DREAD
AUTHOR NAME
THE DRAGONBORN PROPHECY
A BLOODLINE MARKED BY FLAMES
AUTHOR NAME
COVEN OF MIDNIGHT
AUTHOR NAME
COURT OF THE FALLEN THRONE
AUTHOR NAME
THE SERPENT AND THE ROSE
AUTHOR NAME
HOLLOW GATE
AUTHOR NAME
SHATTERED DESTINY
AUTHOR NAME
BLOOD AND BRIARS
AUTHOR NAME
WEB OF BETRAYAL
AUTHOR NAME
QUEEN OF THE CRIMSON BLOOM
AUTHOR NAME
CURSED CROWN
AUTHOR NAME
HEIRESS OF LOVE
AUTHOR NAME
LEGENDS OF THE HIDDEN CITADEL
AUTHOR NAME

ZONEARTZ GRAPHIC DESIGNS

ZoneArtz Graphic Designs offers affordable,
high-quality book covers for authors.
Specializing in fantasy, we also create romance,
sci-fi, action, and more. Need character art?
We've got you covered!

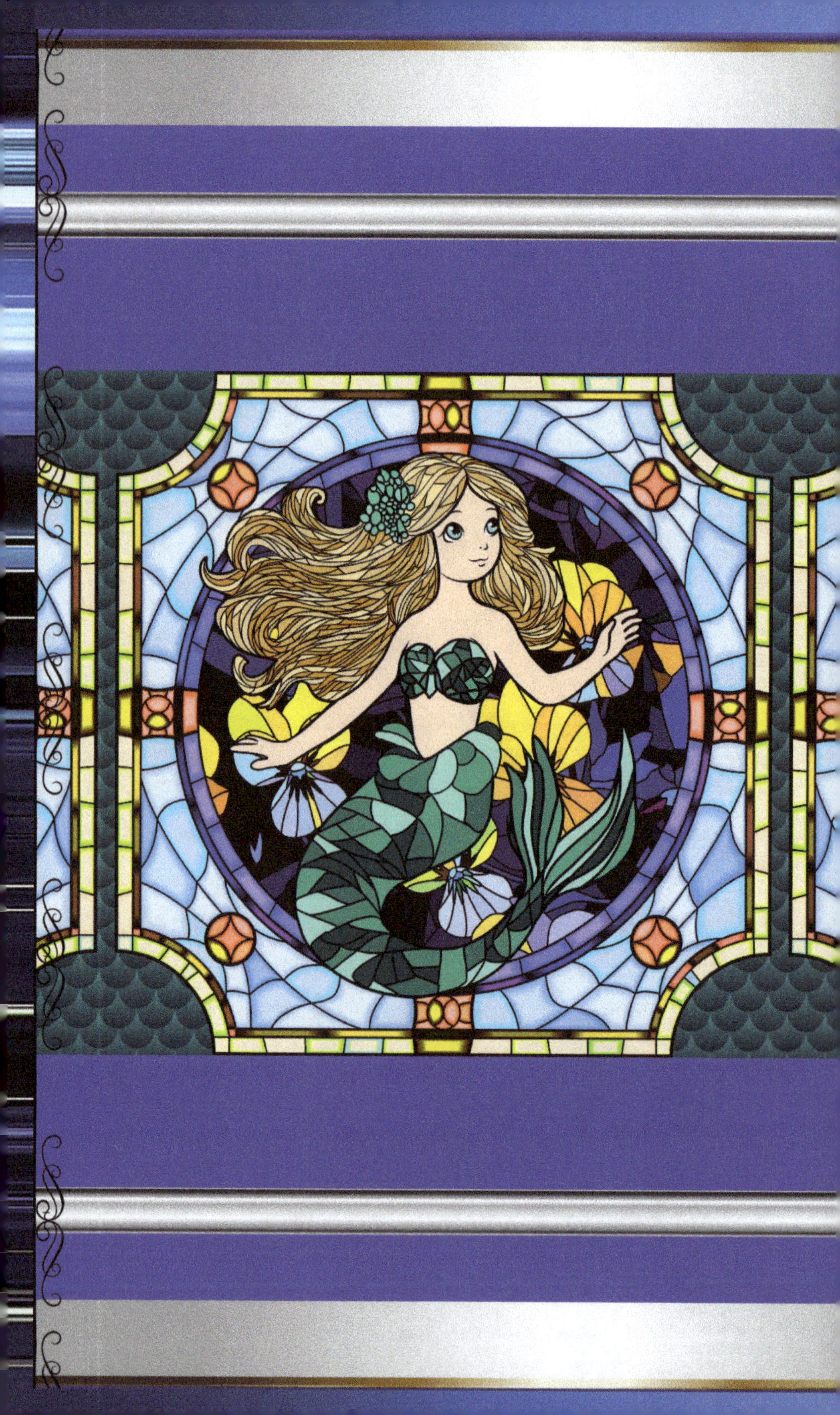

SIREN SECRETS

"Describe a touch that feels like waves—pulling, crashing, consuming. Who do these hands belong to, and how do they make you feel?"

Picture a moment where hands trace your skin like the tide—sometimes gentle, sometimes possessive. What do you feel underneath their touch? Are you safe, or are you being claimed?

BOUND BY THE TIDE

A Dark Mermaid Romance Mad Lib

Instructions: Fill in the blanks first—don't peek ahead!
Then read the story aloud and let the curse consume you.

Fill in the blanks:

1.______________
Adjective (sensual)

2.______________
Body part

3.______________
Verb (past tense)

4.______________
Adjective (forbidden)

5.______________
Body part

6.______________
Body part

7.______________
Sensation (e.g. "pulsing")

8.______________
Adjective

9.______________
Verb (intimate, past tense)

10.______________
Noun (nautical)

11.______________
Sound (pleasurable)

12.______________
Adjective (sinful)

13.______________
Verb (teasing or seductive)

14.______________
Adjective (dangerous or dark)

15.______________
Body part (intimate

16.______________
Emotion (overwhelming)

17.______________
Verb (passion, past tense)

18.______________
Adjective (possessive)

19.______________
Noun (cursed or enchanted)

20.______________
Exclamation (gasp-worthy)

She had once been human. (1)______________, soft, untouched by the sea's cruel grasp—until the witch took everything.

The curse had stolen her breath, her heartbeat, her soul. Now, she was something else. A creature of the deep, driven by hunger.

Her (2)______________ gleamed under the moon as she surfaced, locking onto the shipwrecked man clinging to the waves. The pull of the curse (3)______________ inside her, demanding she take him.

He was perfect. Mortal. (4)______________ in his terror, his (5)______________ trembling as he gasped for air. She reached out, letting the tip of her (6)______________ graze his skin, reveling in the (7)______________ tension between them.

"You shouldn't have come here," she murmured, her voice (8)______________ as the tide. "You should have drowned."

His lips parted, but before he could speak, she (9)______________ against him, the wreckage of his (10)______________ forgotten as the ocean rocked them together.

A (11)______________ escaped him as she kissed him—deep, (12)______________, claiming. Her fingers trailed over his throat. His pulse thundered beneath her touch.

"Beg me," she whispered.

He (13)______________ her name, his body surrendering to her. He was lost now—just like all the others.

She pressed her (14)______________ lips to his (15)______________, letting his (16)______________ seep into her. He tasted like salt and surrender. He was hers.

She (17)______________ him, feeling the curse (18)______________ in her veins as the sea tightened its grip. The (19)______________ sealed their fate.

"(20)______________," he gasped.

And she pulled him under.

Berberis Design

- WORKING ONLY WITH HIGH-QUALITY, LICENSED SOURCES (SUITABLE FOR BOTH PERSONAL AND COMMERCIAL USE);

- DEVELOPMENT OF DESIGNS FOR ALL GENRES IN DIFFERENT STYLES;

- CREATION OF COVERS FOR E-BOOK, PAPERBACK, HARDCOVER;

- SUPPORT AT ALL STAGES OF DESIGN CREATION AND EVEN AFTER (EVEN WHEN THE DESIGN IS APPROVED AND PAID FOR YOU CAN ALWAYS TURN TO MAKE EDITS);

- BOOKING OF DESIGNS (LIKED THE PREMADES, BUT THE BOOK IS NOT READY YET? JUST BOOK IT, AND ALL THE NECESSARY CHANGES WILL BE MADE AT THE ACTUAL TIME);

- IN ADDITION TO COVERS, IT IS ALSO POSSIBLE TO CREATE PROMOTIONAL MATERIALS FOR SOCIAL NETWORKS AND CHANGE CHARACTERS (CLOTHING COLOR, HAIRSTYLES, TATTOOS, ETC.);

- A SYSTEM OF DISCOUNTS FOR REGULAR CUSTOMERS FOR THE SECOND, THIRD AND SUBSEQUENT CUSTOM DESIGNS.

Book series
RUBY RIVARLY
AUTHOR NAME
SAPPHIRE REVENGE
AUTHOR NAME
EMERALD BATTLE
AUTHOR NAME
Hot spicy covers
AUTHOR NAME
GUILTY EASURE
AUTHOR NAME
Inner ESSENCE
OF STE
WHEN I WAS WITH YOU
A LOVE HATE STORY
AUTHOR NAME
BITTEN
Author Name
Illustrative cov
Author Name
TALES of the MERMAID
Fantasy covers
Fatal Nigt
AUTHOR NAME
ARROW FATE
AUTHOR NAME
POSEID REVENG
AUTHOR'S NAME

Tails Tell
Ancient Tales

Covers & Berries

SIREN SECRETS

"Write about a kiss that feels like being lost at sea—intoxicating, dangerous, inescapable. Who is kissing you, and what do they want?"

Describe a kiss that takes something from you—your breath, your thoughts, your control.
What does it awaken in you?
Do you fight it, or do you let yourself drown?

Cyan Book
Cover Designs

SIREN SECRETS

"Describe a love that tastes like
salt, sin, and something dark.
What are you willing to do to keep it?"

Your lover is dangerous—maybe
even monstrous—but you love him anyway.
What does that love feel like? How does it taste?
What price would you pay to never lose it?

REFLECTION

How far would you go
for love?

Do you believe love
should be safe, or
should it be wild and
dangerous?

What's the darkest
thought you've had
about keeping
someone close?

HI, I'M JHEA, ALSO KNOWN AS *OBSI ART*, I'VE BEEN DESIGNING BOOK COVERS FOR OVER SEVEN YEARS. MY MAIN EXPERTISE IS IN FANTASY, CONTEMPORARY ROMANCE, AND SCI-FI COVERS, BUT I AM VERSITILE AND CAN WORK WITH VARIOUS GENRES AS WELL.

Services

BOOK COVER

BOOK EDGE DESIGNS

INTERIOR DESIGNS
colored/b&w | chapter header & break

CARTOGRAPHY

CHARACTER/ NSFW ART

OTHER SERVICES:
- AUTHOR BRANDING
- GRAPHIC DESIGNS
- MERCHANDISE DESIGNS (BOOKMARK, HOODIES, TUMBLER, ETC..)

LUNA'S
Protector
AUTHOR NAME

Entangled
AUTHOR NAME

AUTHOR NAME
The
AWAKENING
DRAGONBOUND

AUTHOR NAME
OBSI ART - PREMADE and CUSTOM DESIGN
SWAN
Syndicate

LOVE, LOYALTY, AND BETRAYAL
MAFIA
Triad
OBSI ART - PREMADE AND CUSTOM COVER DESIGN
AUTHOR NAME

CELESTIAL
BONDS
AUTHOR NAME

SIREN SECRETS

"Describe the pull of the ocean. What does it whisper to you? Is it a call of love, danger, or something more primal?"

Imagine standing at the edge of the sea, the waves lapping at your feet. What would happen if you walked forward? Would you sink, swim, or be claimed by something waiting beneath?

REFLECTION

Have you ever felt drawn to something mysterious, even if it was dangerous?

What do you crave that feels out of reach, like the deep unknown?

If the ocean represents emotion, what feelings threaten to pull you under?

RF
Creatives

SIREN SECRETS

"A man washes ashore with no memory except your name on his lips. Who is he to you?"

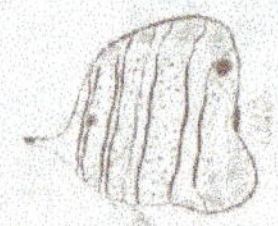

Describe the first time you touch him. Does his body remember what his mind has forgotten?

Taken by the Tide

A Dark Mermaid Romance Mad Lib

Instructions: Fill in the blanks first—don't peek ahead!
Then read it aloud and let the waves of desire pull you under.

Fill in the blanks:

1.___________
Adjective (sensual)
2.___________
Body part (erotic)
3.___________
Verb (past tense, intimate)
4.___________
Adjective (forbidden)
5.___________
Body part (sensitive)
6.___________
Object (intimate)
7.___________
Sensation (e.g. "pulsing")
8.___________
Adjective (wet or slippery)
9.___________
Verb (intimate, past tense)
10.___________
Noun (nautical)
11.___________
Sound (pleasurable)
12.___________
Adjective (sinful)
13.___________
Verb (teasing or seductive)
14.___________
djective (dangerous or dark)
15.___________
Body part (intimate
16.___________
Emotion (overwhelming)
17.___________
Verb (passion, past tense)
18.___________
Adjective (possessive)
19.___________
Noun (cursed or enchanted)
20.___________
Exclamation (gasp-worthy)

The water was (1)___________ as they pulled the drowning figure beneath the waves, her (2)___________ brushing against his trembling skin. He had barely (3)___________ before he was caught—trapped in a (4)___________ embrace.

His (5)___________ throbbed as cool fingers traced his flesh, the ocean wrapping around them like a lover's grip. Something (6)___________ pressed into him, teasing, tormenting, making his body burn with (7)___________ need.

"You don't fear me, do you?" the siren purred, her (8)___________ lips ghosting over his pulse.

A moan escaped him as he (9)___________ into her touch, letting the salt and silk of her consume him. He should have feared this, should have fought, but he was already sinking—into the (10)___________, into her.

She made a (11)___________ sound, a warning, a promise. "Be careful, sailor. I bite."

The way she (12)___________ ran her tongue over his skin made his restraint shatter. He (13)___________ her name, hands roaming the length of her, claiming what should never be his.

Something (14)___________ flickered in her gaze before she pulled him deeper, pressing against his (15)___________, dragging him into the abyss of (16)___________.

"Tell me you want this," she whispered, and when he (17)___________ her back, it was with the force of a storm crashing against the shore.

The water trembled around them, the very ocean bending to their pleasure. The siren knew— he was already lost. Not just to the sea.

But to the (18)___________, unbreakable (19)___________ that bound them together.

"(20)___________," he gasped, and the ocean swallowed them whole.

SIREN SECRETS

"The waves crash violently around you as he pulls you close. The storm rages, but so does your longing. Do you surrender?"

Have you ever felt a love or desire as intense as a storm?

What does it mean to let go completely?

Does passion burn brighter in chaos or in calm?

Capture the heat, the desperation, the taste of salt and danger on his lips.

FEELINGS WORD SEARCH

```
K F Y H P O W E R E L F E R F
R A Z Z G C C V F U R Y F X T
P R M S F A A F E Q T P Q O Y
F S U R R E N D E R Q V R I T
G L H L E C I F I R C A S E L
T A A V H C B G J Y C S I R A
G Y Y T B H H A N M U X E N Y
B A J E L L I O I I Y X A D O
V R M A D N O M I R G B S G L
C T F E D J J I P C I N V S W
M E J E M U X B U Q E D O D G
U B Y S I O X E H G Y I C L W
T F Z Q Q R R K Z K T B K V X
T P M V R N G Y B L B C M Z K
N N O I T P M E D E R R A E F
```

BETRAYAL   FURY   LOYALTY   REDEMPTION
CHOICE   GRIEF   MEMORY   SACRIFICE
FEAR   LONGING   POWER   SURRENDER

ELF
PRINCE

ICE
age

AUTHOR NAME
SWORD
OF THE
DEATH

AUTHOR NAME
ONCE
UPON
A
BOOK

AUTHOR NAME
OF FIRE
AND ICE

AUTHOR NAME
DEMON'S
PURSUIT

OTHER
HALF

AUTHOR NAME
TALE OF A
MERMAN'S
TAIL

Meet Athena Crest Arts!

Athena Crest Arts brings your stories to life with stunning and affordable book covers! Specializing in epic fantasy, young adult, and typographical designs, we craft visuals that captivate readers at first glance. Now expanding into illustrated book covers and character art, we're here to elevate your book's creative appeal.

Need a custom cover or artwork for your next masterpiece? Let's make magic together! ✨

Mermaid
VIBES

Land Word Search

Y M R O T S U R E E F H X H H
I O Y K X Y Q R I T I Z U C Z
U N I U E C H W I S L A N G K
D A Z N O E W Y L P C E Z C H
M I S T Q Q S A U Y R P C L T
F H Q B L I N Z G T H A A H U
E J G I L D S L L M V R G T P
G S Z E A J O G S E O I S N I
T M N W X W P T R C L O H E Q
X C G I E X W N F N E Y A R G
E C C S Q F X M O E R M D R J
Y M N N I A R O T H E Z O U C
Z Q O V H M M V F I T N W C E
X T M V U X F H N N G B S I S
Y E W X B F I R E L I G H T A

CAVERN	GLOW	RAIN	STORM
CORAL	ISLAND	REEF	TRENCH
CURRENT	MIST	SHADOWS	
FIRELIGHT	MOONLIGHT	SILENCE	

HI, THIS IS LUNEAESTHETE DESIGNS.

A GRAPHIC DESIGNER OF 4 YEARS. HERE TO HELP YOU BRING YOUR STORIES TO LIFE, WITH AN AFFORABLE-PRICE. SPECIALIZING IN BOOK COVERS.
I DO ANY GENRE BUT MAINLY DOING FANTASY AND DARK-ROMANCE COVERS.
I ALSO OFFER ILLUSTRATED CHARACTER ARTS BOTH NORMAL ONES AND NSFW.

IF INTERESTED IN WORKING WITH ME, YOU CAN FIND ME ON MY FACEBOOK GROUP OR EMAIL ME DIRECTLY.

FB: LUNEAESTHETE DESIGNS
EMAIL: LUNEAESTHETEDESIGNS@GMAIL.COM

AUTHOR NAME
MOONLIT HAUNTING

AUTHOR NAME
THE PHEONIX'S CHOSEN

AUTHOR NAME
WHERE SHADOWS COLLIDE

SCALES OF THE STARBOUND
AUTHOR NAME

AUTHOR NAME
SERIES TITLE HERE BOOK
BALLAD OF THE SIREN

AUTHOR NAME
Inked Lies

AUTHOR NAME
SWEET MISTAKE
SERIES TITLE HERE
BOOK 1

AUTHOR NAME
CURSED QUEEN

AUTHOR NAME
THE BREAK-UP LIST
SERIES TITLE HERE
BOOK 1

SIREN SECRETS

"If you had to give up your voice, your freedom, or your heart in exchange for one unforgettable night of desire, which would you surrender?"

A dark figure offers you a choice—your voice, your freedom, or your heart in exchange for a night of passion that will haunt you forever.
What do you choose, and why?

XIELLE COVERS

EST 2025

SAMPLE WORKS:

Xielle Covers is a creative design studi
launched in 2025 specializing in boo
covers and character arts. We'r
passionate about bringing stories to lif
through captivating designs, fro
fiction to fantasy and beyon

SIREN SECRETS

Explore the feeling of recognition
between two souls drawn together by the sea.

REFLECTION

Have you ever met someone who felt like home?

Do you believe in instant, magnetic attraction?

What does it mean to find someone who understands your darkness?

GEKA

GRAPHICS BY GEKA

Hi! My name is Geka, a graphic designer, and the owner Graphics by Geka - Premade Book Covers & Other Graphics specialized in dark and fantasy covers, but I could also do vari genres and cover types. Thus, Graphics by Geka off affordable, yet quality covers.

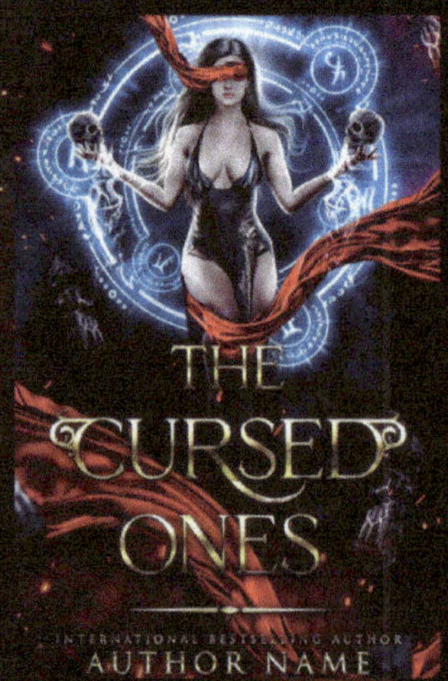

SERVICES

BOOK COVER

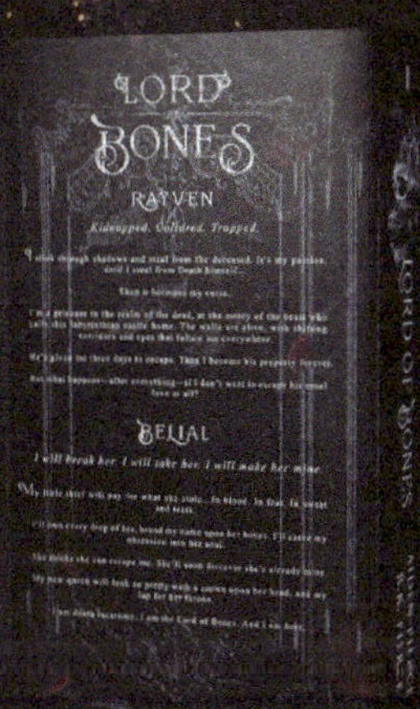

INTERIOR

OTHER SERVICES:

- BOOKMARKS
- BOOK TRAILER
- LOGO DESIGN
- STICKERS
- PROMOTIONAL MATERIALS
- CHIBIS
- ETC.

Come, Dear Sailor

SIREN SECRETS

"Every time you try to leave the ocean, something pulls you back. What is it—love, magic, or a curse?"

Describe your final attempt to leave.
Does the sea win, or do you?

REFLECTION

Is there something in your life you keep returning to, even when you try to let it go?

Do you believe we can ever truly escape our fate?

What does the ocean represent to you— freedom, captivity, or something else?

THE CALL OF THE DEEP

A Dark Mermaid Romance Mad Lib

Instructions: Fill in the blanks first—don't peek ahead!
Then read it aloud and let the ocean take you.

Fill in the blanks:

1. _______________
Adjective (haunting or eerie)

2. _______________
Body part (exposed)

3. _______________
Sensation (e.g. "aching")

4. _______________
Adjective (forbidden)

5. _______________
Noun (natural element)

6. _______________
Sound

7. _______________
Adjective

8. _______________
Verb (past tense)

9. _______________
Body part (intimate)

10. _______________
Noun (cursed or enchanted)

11. _______________
Adjective (wet or slippery)

12. _______________
Verb (past tense)

13. _______________
Emotion (overwhelming)

14. _______________
Body part (sensitive)

15. _______________
Verb (past tense)

16. _______________
Adjective (possessive)

17. _______________
Exclamation

The sea was calling him again. The wind carried something (1)_______________ through the night—something that slithered into his ears and settled beneath his skin.

He stood at the edge of the ship, the salt stinging his (2)_______________, the endless water stretching before him. It pulsed with (3)_______________ need, a whisper just beneath the waves. "Come closer."

His captain had warned him of the (4)_______________ things that lurked in the deep. The way the (5)_______________ could take hold of a man, drag him under.

But the sound—(6)_______________, seductive—wrapped around him like a lover's breath. "You belong to me."

His fingers trembled as he leaned forward, the ocean growing darker, deeper. (7)_______________. He had never been afraid of the sea before, but this... this was different.

The voice (8)_______________ through him, curling against his spine, tracing over his (9)_______________ like unseen hands. "Let go."

Something glowed beneath the surface—a (10)_______________, shifting, waiting. He swayed. The ship felt unsteady, the deck (11)_______________ beneath his feet.

He (12)_______________ as unseen fingers dragged over his mind, his will bending, breaking.

The pull was stronger now, thick with (13)_______________. He swallowed hard, his (14)_______________ throbbing with something he didn't understand. "I will have you." And then—he (15)_______________ forward.

The sea caught him in its (16)_______________ embrace, swallowing him whole.

The last thing he saw before the darkness claimed him was the shape beneath the waves, waiting. The last thing he heard was the voice, whispering against his skin— "Welcome home."

"(17)_______________," he gasped—before the ocean pulled him under.

SIREN SECRETS

"You have lived on land, but the ocean calls you back. A lover waits in both places. Who do you choose?"

Picture the moment you must decide.
Do you step onto the shore or into the waves?

REFLECTION

Have you ever felt torn between two versions of yourself?

What does home mean to you—people, places, or something deeper?

Do you chase comfort, or do you crave the unknown?

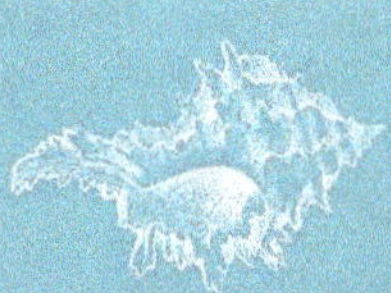

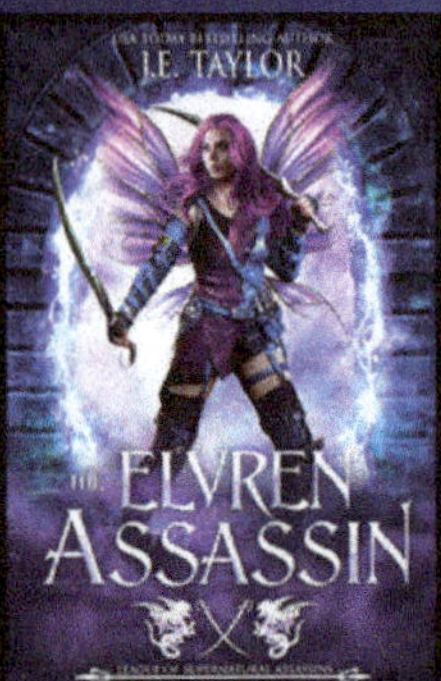
USA TODAY BESTSELLING AUTHOR
J.E. TAYLOR
THE ELVREN ASSASSIN
LEAGUE OF SUPERNATURAL ASSASSINS

SLM CREATIONS
BETA
HEARTS OF BLUE

THE FORGOTTEN
CLANS

STITCHED UNDER FIRE
USA TODAY BESTSELLING AUTHOR
CASSIDY K. O'CONNOR AND SHERI LYN

SLM CREATIONS
CYBER STALKED
OFFENSIVE ACTION

SLM CREATIONS
MOON STRUCK
SHIFTER UNIVERSE

SLM CREATIONS
DRAGON HEART
SHIFTER UNIVERSE

SLM CREATIONS
SCORCHED STRIPES
SHIFTER UNIVERSE

SLM CREATIONS
THUNDER STORM
SHIFTER UNIVERSE

SLM CREATIONS
FIRE WINGS
SHIFTER UNIVERSE

SLM CREATIONS
FOX TRAIL
SHIFTER UNIVERSE

SLM CREATIONS
BEAR RIDGE
SHIFTER UNIVERSE

SLM CREATIONS
SPOTTED CLAWS
SHIFTER UNIVERSE

Taming the ALIEN
SLM CREATIONS

SLM CREATIONS
HEXES and CURSES

SLM CREATIONS
HIDDEN CURSES

SLM CREATIONS
SHADY CURSES

SLM CREATIONS
DRAGON FLIGHT

TIME BREACH
PORTAL KEEPERS
SLM CREATIONS

TIME JUMPERS
PORTAL KEEPERS
SLM CREATIONS

TIMED DESTINATION
PORTAL KEEPERS
SLM CREATIONS

I'm Sheri-Lynn Marean of SLM Creations, and I'm an author and artist.

I began drawing at 12 years old, mostly animals but really anything that caught my fancy. Over the years, I've sold original drawings, paintings, limited edition prints … I'm also a published paranormal and fantasy romance author and learned how to create in Photoshop in order to make my own book covers.

I quickly realized that I loved creating pretty digital art, and I wanted to do so for other authors.

I'm always learning and trying to improve my skills, and currently offer custom & pre-made book covers in the paranormal romance, fantasy, urban fantasy, dystopian, and sci-fi romance genres. I've recently branched out to include interior chapter art, painted edges, and character art via a mix of photo manipulation and over-painting.

SIREN SECRETS

"You are drowning, but a lover's arms wrap around you. At first, you think he's saving you. Then you realize—he's taking you deeper."

Describe the moment you realize you're not being saved. Do you fight, or do you let go?

REFLECTION

Have you ever trusted someone completely, only to question it too late?

What does surrender feel like—peaceful or terrifying?

Do you believe in fate, or Is love a choice?

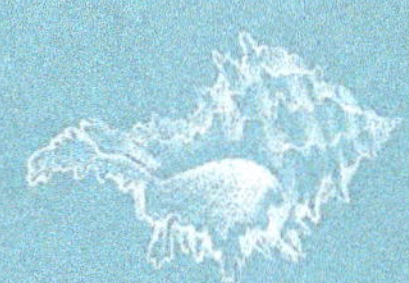

The Impossible Reunion

The Thatian wind felt different from the sea breeze I'd known before. It was warmer, dustier, laced with the scent of wild citrus trees and worn cobblestones. We walked the last stretch on foot, the carriage unable to manage the narrow streets that wound through the heart of the village. My boots crunched against gravel as we climbed the hill toward the home where my sister now lived.

I hadn't seen it in years.

The town hadn't changed much. Cracked shutters still swung from crooked windows. The baker still left baskets out for the stray cats. Children darted through alleyways like windblown leaves, but every corner felt haunted by a younger version of myself—the one who had dreamed of something better and ended up dragged into something worse.

Elios walked beside me, his hand warm in mine. He hadn't let go once since we arrived.

"Azure," he said gently, "you don't have to be afraid."

I didn't answer. I couldn't. My throat had gone tight from the weight of everything I wanted to say and wasn't sure how to. What if she hated me for leaving? What if she didn't remember? What if the little girl I'd died to protect didn't want me now that I was alive again?

The building came into view.

It was modest—a washed stone house tucked between two weather worn garden walls. Ivy crawled across its base, and a worn wooden sign swung above the door: *Safe haven House*. It didn't look like much, but it had kept her safe, and that mattered more than anything.

My heart thundered as I stepped up to the door. Before I could knock, it opened.

A woman stood there, gray-haired and sun-browned, a toddler cradled on her hip. Her eyes swept over us, wary but not unkind.

"Can I help you?"

Swallowing back my hesitation, I stepped forward. "My name is Azure. I'm looking for my sister. Daneliya. I believe she's in your care."

The woman stared at me for a long moment. Something in her expression shifted—recognition, maybe, or disbelief.

"She never stopped talking about you," she said, her body language instantly changing to something more welcoming. "Come in."

She led us through a warm hallway that smelled of soap and something sweet baking in the kitchen. A few children peeked at us from behind door frames, curious and wide-eyed. The woman stopped at a sunlit room at the end of the hall and tapped gently on the door frame.

"Daneliya," she said softly, "you have visitors."

The girl who turned looked nothing like the small child I'd left behind.

She was nearly as tall as me now, her frame still narrow but her face older and sharper. Her hair was pulled back in a braid, and she wore a simple cotton dress with bare feet, which reminded me so much of my friend. Thinking about Ocevia only made the emotions brewing inside me more potent.

For a moment, my little sister just stared at me, her dark eyes wide. I didn't know what to say, but then her lips parted, and when she spoke, her voice trembled. "Azure?"

I nodded, too afraid to speak, but she moved fast, throwing all my hesitation to the wind.

In seconds, she crossed the room and threw herself into my arms, her sobs breaking open like a storm.

I dropped to my knees to hold her, wrapping both arms around her shaking body just like I had on the beach all those years ago. Her tears soaked my shoulder, and mine were already falling.

"I thought you were dead," she cried. "I thought I'd never see you again."

"I tried to come back sooner," I whispered, pressing my lips to her hair. "I swear I did. But I'm here now. I'm here."

Kneeling beside us, Elios rested a hand gently on Daneliya's back. She didn't flinch. She didn't even look up. She just held on tighter, as if afraid I might disappear again, but I wasn't going anywhere.

Not this time.

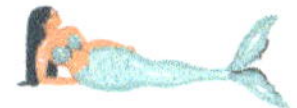

Later, we sat together on the edge of the small garden behind Safe haven, where fig trees leaned toward the sun and vines crept between the stones. Only the occasional birdsong or the distant laughter of other children inside broke the quiet. Daneliya sat between us, her hand still looped through mine like she was afraid I might vanish if she let go.

I studied her in the golden light. I saw traces of the child I remembered—the roundness of her cheeks, the way her nose crinkled when she smiled—but she had grown. There was something older in her eyes. Something I recognized all too well.

"I used to come out here when I missed you," she said softly, her feet swinging beneath her. "I'd sit under that tree and imagine you walking up the hill." Her fingers tightened around mine. "I stopped after a while. I thought maybe I was imagining someone who'd never come back."

My chest tightened, heart breaking. "I should have come sooner."

"You came," she whispered, smiling up at me. "That's all that matters."

Elios glanced between us, then leaned forward slightly. "We didn't just come to visit."

Daneliya looked up at him, brows lifting.

I reached into the small satchel at my side and pulled out a sealed envelope. Inside was a letter from the Thatia council, formally recognizing our adoption of her, if she wanted it. I handed it to her, but she didn't open it—just looked at me with wide, cautious eyes.

"I want you to come home with us," I said. "To Starspell."

She blinked, and for a heartbeat, I saw every emotion pass through her—hope, disbelief, fear, joy—all tumbling through her expression like waves crashing against the shore.

"You would live with us," Elios added. "Go to school. Have your own room. Anything you need."

"I..." Her voice broke. She looked down at the letter in her hands, then up at me again. "Do you really want me?"

Tears blurred my vision, but I couldn't help but smile. "You're my sister. Of course I want you."

She didn't answer right away. Her lip trembled, and she ducked her head, nodding once, twice, before throwing herself into my arms again.

"I'd like that," she said. "I'd really like that."

Elios leaned into the hug, his arms circling around both of us. For the first time in years, we weren't scattered pieces of a broken family. We were together. We were whole.

And this time, we were going home.

We left Thatia the next morning beneath a sky painted in soft lilac and rose, the kind of dawn that felt like a blessing. The wind off the bay was calm, catching gently in the sails as our ship cut through the waves. Daneliya stood between us at the railing, her hands gripping the edge as she watched the sea roll past with wide, wandering eyes.

She hadn't said much since we boarded, but she hadn't let go of my hand either. I didn't push her. There would be time for questions later—about where I'd been, what I'd become, what she had lived through while I was gone.

But not yet. This moment wasn't for history. It was for something quieter. Something new.

Elios leaned against the railing beside her, his arm brushing mine as the morning light caught in his hair. He looked out toward the horizon, his gaze far away, but his presence steady as ever.

"I think you'll like Starspell," he said softly. "There's a tree that blooms just outside the window. And a pond full of frogs that croak all night."

Daneliya cracked a smile, small but real. "Do the frogs sing?"

Elios grinned. "Only off-key."

Giggling, she glanced up at me, her smile softening. "Are we really going to live there?"

"If you want to," I said. "We're not just taking you. We're choosing you."

She was quiet for a long time. Then she nodded, eyes fixed on the sea. "I want that."

We stood together at the bow as the ship carried us forward. No chains, no gods, no curses. Just a girl who had waited too long, a sister who had fought her way home, and the man who had helped make that home possible.

I didn't know what the future would hold, but I knew this: we were no longer survivors of a broken past. We were the beginning of something whole.

And for the first time in years, I let myself believe we were finally free.

SIREN SECRETS

"A sailor binds himself to the mast to resist your song, but his eyes betray his longing. Do you let him go, or do you claim him?"

Describe his struggle—not just against the ropes, but against his desire for you. How does it make you feel?

SIREN SECRETS

"You were taken aboard his ship, but instead
of fear, you feel something else—
an unsettling, undeniable pull. He watches
you like you belong to him. Do you?"

Describe the moment he locks eyes with you.
Is there a promise in them... or a warning?

REFLECTION

Have you ever felt
drawn to someone in
a way you couldn't
explain?

What does obsession
mean to you—love,
control, or something
else?

Would you rather be
desired fiercely or
loved gently?

For over two decades,
Timothy Higgins of Swampy Sloth Studios
has been crafting exceptional artwork,
both digital and traditional.

Specializing in:

Book covers

Immersive interior art and Design

Character book-accurate designs

Authors branding

Merchandising design / promotional artwork

Book edge designs

Comic Book Art and storytelling

From horror to the passionate realms of romance (including NSFW), the imaginative genres of historical, fantasy, and science fiction, Swampy Sloth Studios expertly translates your vision into compelling visuals.

If you want your vision realized with precision and passion, Let Swampy Sloth Studios be your artistic Partner!

WWW.SWAMPSLOTH.COM
THE GOLDEN AWAKENING
Hot &
Steamy
PORTLAND
2024

SIREN SECRETS

"Under the full moon, your reflection in the water shifts—you are not human anymore. What are you? How do you feel?"

Describe the sensation of your body changing. Is it painful, freeing, or both?

REFLECTION

Have you ever felt like you were meant to be something other than what you are?

What part of yourself do you hide from the world?

If you could transform, would you ever want to change back?

Welcome to LEIGH GRAPHIC DESIGNS
by LEIGH CADIENTE

We are a creative graphic design team specializing in bringing your literary visions to life through stunning visuals. We have been operating for 5 years in the industry! At Leigh Graphic Designs, we are passionate about crafting book covers that captivate and draw readers in, designing character illustrations that give life to your stories, and creating inside book layouts that make every page an experience.

We also cater to NSFW arts, ensuring tasteful and expressive designs tailored to your specific needs, as well as book edge designs that add a unique, eye-catching touch to your printed works. Our team is dedicated to delivering high-quality, customized designs that reflect your vision and connect with your audience.

With a blend of creativity, skill, and attention to detail, we bring your ideas to life in ways that stand out. Whether you're an author, publisher, or just in need of creative designs, we're here to help make your project unforgettable.

Let's collaborate and create something amazing!

SIREN SECRETS

"A ship crashes against the rocks, and among the wreckage, you find a survivor— one you loved and lost long ago."

Describe the moment your eyes meet. Do you rescue him... or let the sea finish what it started?

REFLECTION

Have you ever been faced with someone from your past you thought you'd never see again?

What would you say if you were given one last chance with a lost love?

Is it possible to rebuild what has been shattered?

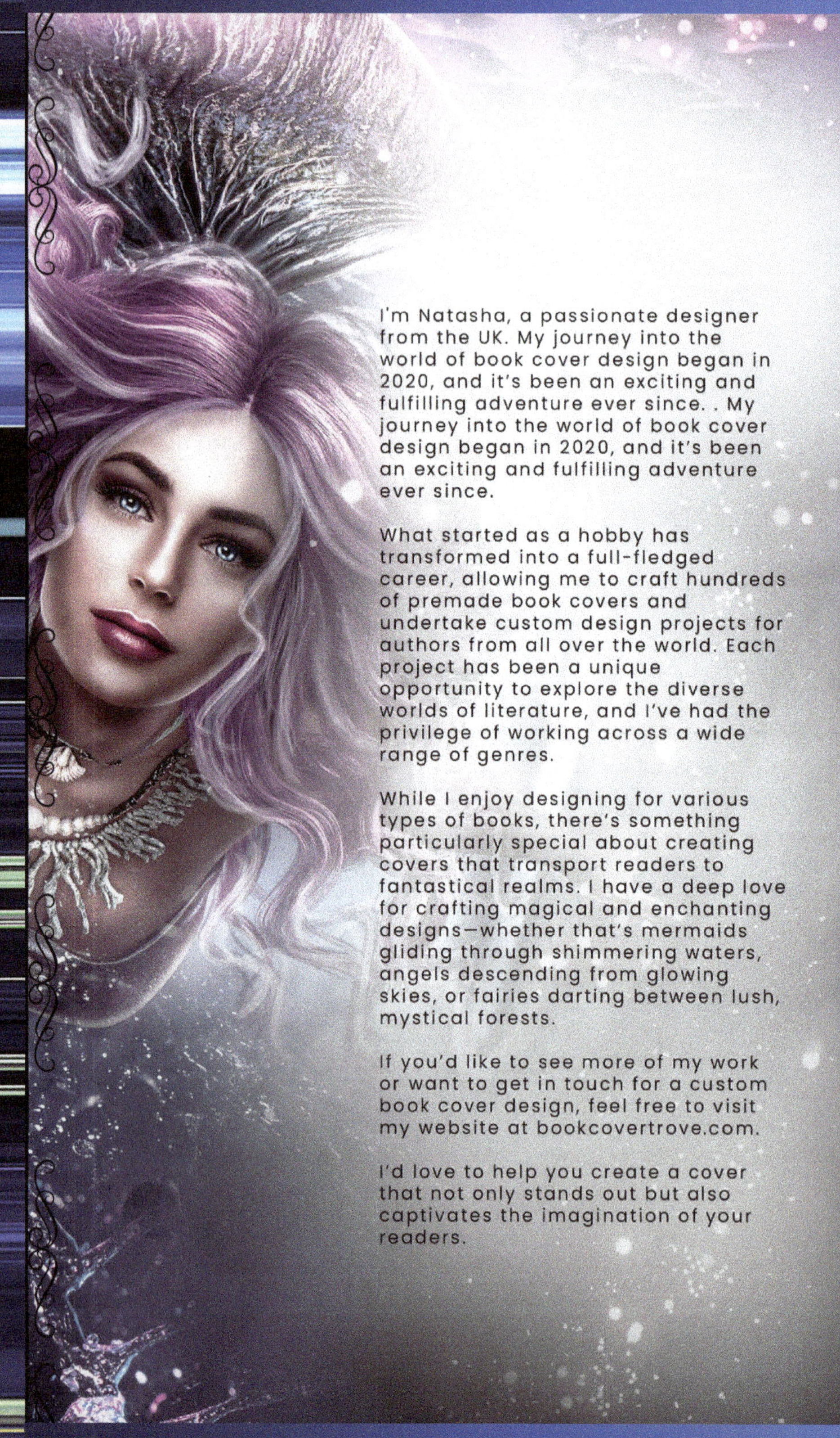

I'm Natasha, a passionate designer from the UK. My journey into the world of book cover design began in 2020, and it's been an exciting and fulfilling adventure ever since. . My journey into the world of book cover design began in 2020, and it's been an exciting and fulfilling adventure ever since.

What started as a hobby has transformed into a full-fledged career, allowing me to craft hundreds of premade book covers and undertake custom design projects for authors from all over the world. Each project has been a unique opportunity to explore the diverse worlds of literature, and I've had the privilege of working across a wide range of genres.

While I enjoy designing for various types of books, there's something particularly special about creating covers that transport readers to fantastical realms. I have a deep love for crafting magical and enchanting designs—whether that's mermaids gliding through shimmering waters, angels descending from glowing skies, or fairies darting between lush, mystical forests.

If you'd like to see more of my work or want to get in touch for a custom book cover design, feel free to visit my website at bookcovertrove.com.

I'd love to help you create a cover that not only stands out but also captivates the imagination of your readers.

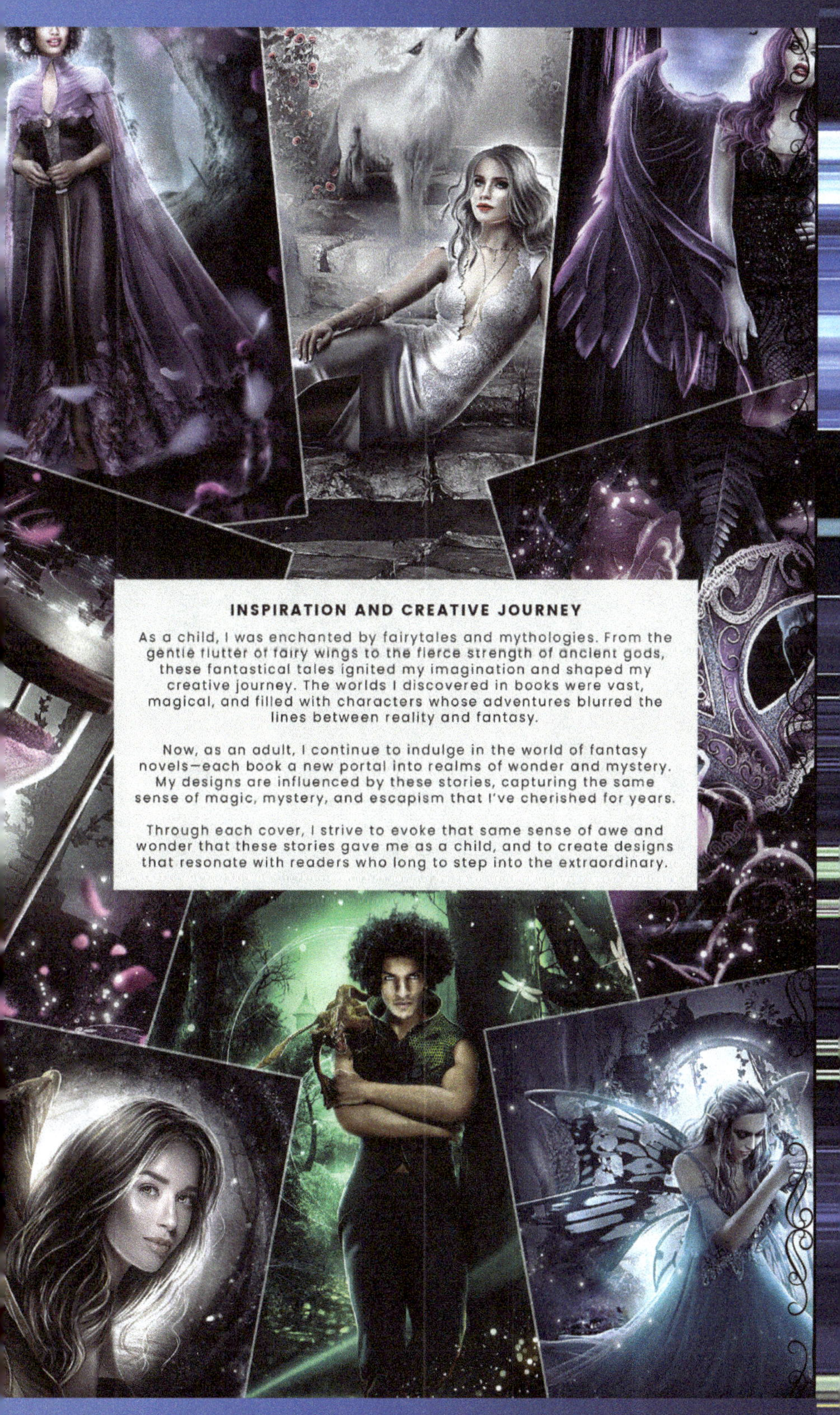

INSPIRATION AND CREATIVE JOURNEY

As a child, I was enchanted by fairytales and mythologies. From the gentle flutter of fairy wings to the fierce strength of ancient gods, these fantastical tales ignited my imagination and shaped my creative journey. The worlds I discovered in books were vast, magical, and filled with characters whose adventures blurred the lines between reality and fantasy.

Now, as an adult, I continue to indulge in the world of fantasy novels—each book a new portal into realms of wonder and mystery. My designs are influenced by these stories, capturing the same sense of magic, mystery, and escapism that I've cherished for years.

Through each cover, I strive to evoke that same sense of awe and wonder that these stories gave me as a child, and to create designs that resonate with readers who long to step into the extraordinary.

Achlys
Book Cover
Designs

The ocean
remembers
her name

SIREN SECRETS

"A storm rages, and a voice whispers to you from the sea, promising love and power if you surrender yourself. Do you take the offer?"

Imagine stepping into the waves, the water rising around you as the voice grows clearer. What happens next?

REFLECTION

What would you sacrifice for the love you desire?

Have you ever been tempted by something that felt both dangerous and irresistible?

What does surrender mean to you— freedom or captivity?

GCAT DESIGNS
AUTHOR NAME
MOONLIT WHISPERS

HOUSE OF DESCENDANTS SERIES
STRANGE LEGACY
DESIGN BY GIGI CREATIVES
AUTHOR NAME

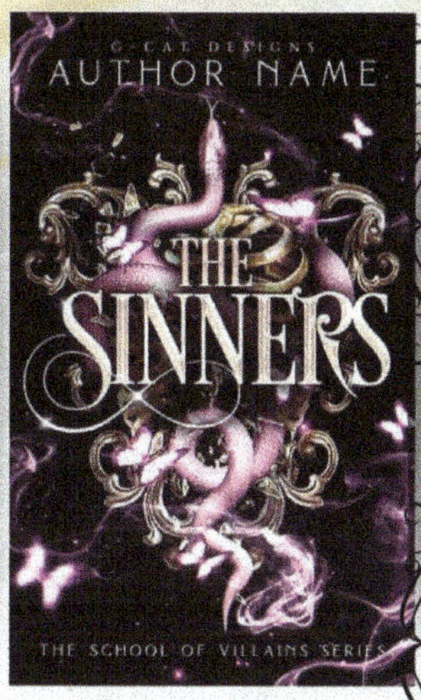
G-CAT DESIGNS
AUTHOR NAME
THE SINNERS
THE SCHOOL OF VILLAINS SERIES

G-CAT DESIGNS
AUTHOR NAME
BLOOD OF THE DJINN
A TALES OF MAGIC BETRAYALS

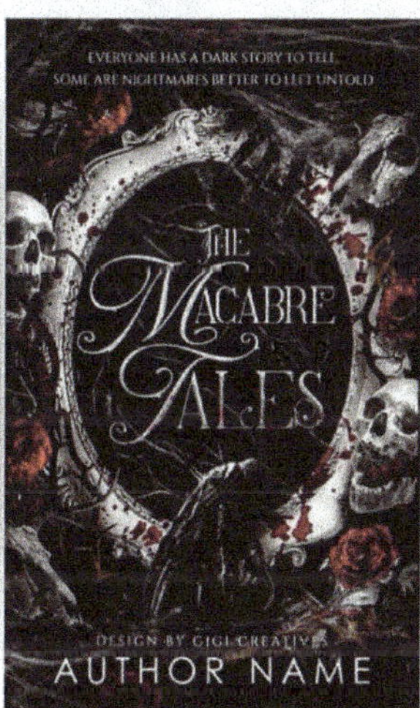
EVERYONE HAS A DARK STORY TO TELL
SOME ARE NIGHTMARES BETTER TO LEFT UNTOLD
THE MACABRE TALES
DESIGN BY GIGI CREATIVES
AUTHOR NAME

AFFAIRS AND DEATH BOOK ONE
INNATE POISON
DESIGN BY GIGI CREATIVES
AUTHOR NAME

HOUSE OF THE FIFTH DRAGON SERIES
THE WYVERN PRINCE
DESIGN BY GIGI CREATIVES
AUTHOR NAME

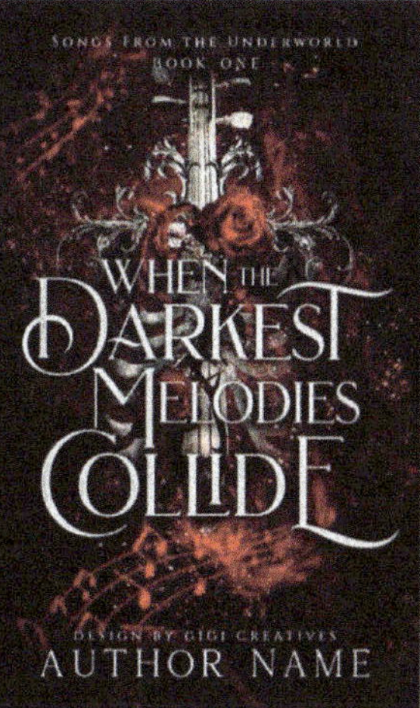
SONGS FROM THE UNDERWORLD BOOK ONE
WHEN THE DARKEST MELODIES COLLIDE
DESIGN BY GIGI CREATIVES
AUTHOR NAME

WICKED CINDERELLA
A DESIRE IS A FANTASY YOUR MIND MAKES
DESIGN BY GIGI CREATIVES
AUTHOR NAME

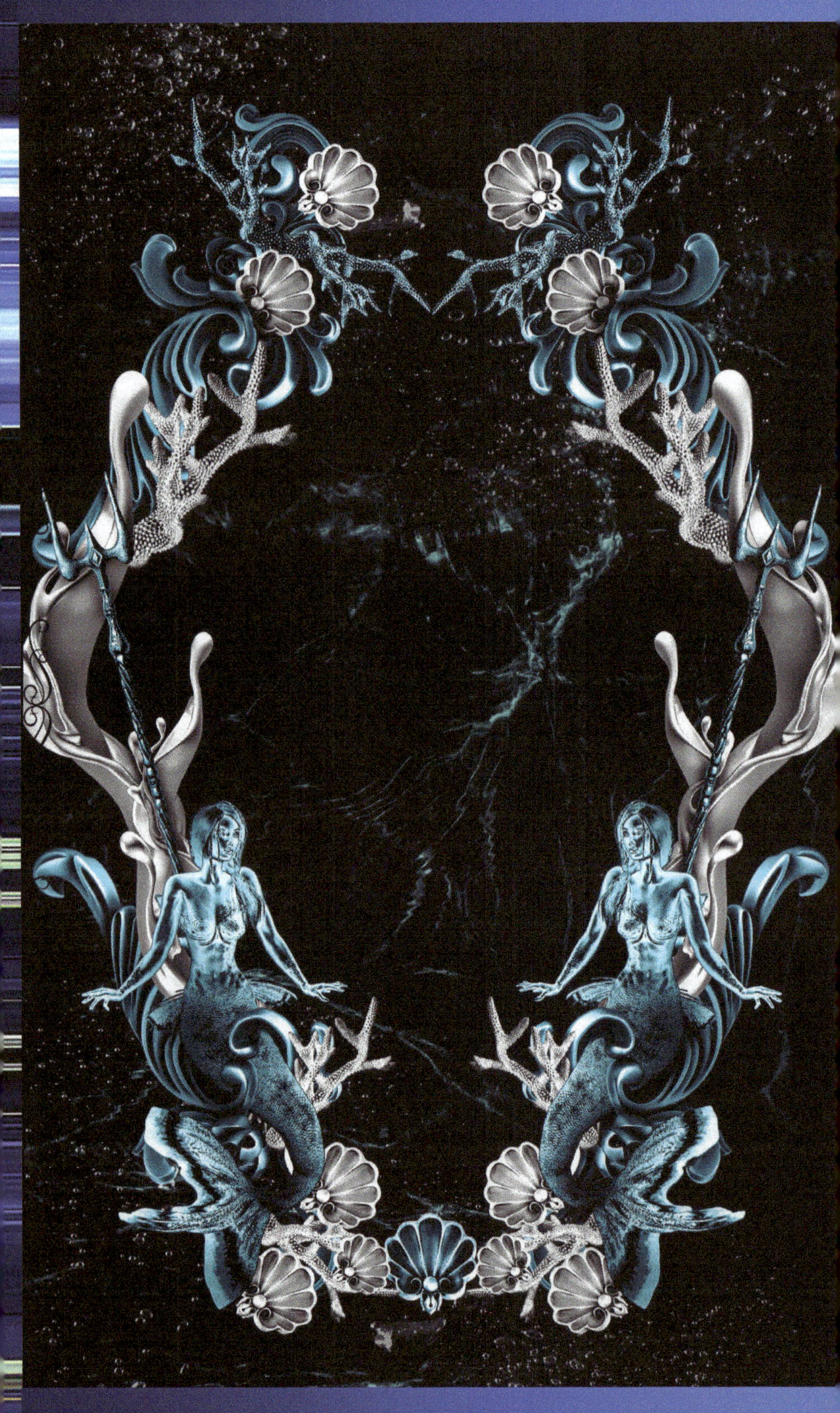

Various Artists
& Designers

Tatiana Mitrushova

Alvindo

BarvArt

Atky

J Horrocks

xoxo
ATKY

FROM THE EVERETT
COLLECTION

Fernando Cortes

Designer Candies

SIREN SECRETS

"He offers you something rare from the ocean
depths, pressing it into your hand like a promise.
But treasures always come at a cost."

Describe the pearl. Is it warm, pulsing, alive?
What happens when you accept it?

SIREN SECRETS

"Imagine being in love with someone who fears what you are. Would you reveal your true nature, or would you drag them into the depths?"

Imagine looking into the eyes of someone who adores you—until they see the real you.
Do they run, or do they reach for you anyway?
Would you pull them deeper, even if it meant they'd never return?

REFLECTION

Have you ever hidden parts of yourself to make someone love you?

What part of you feels "too much" for others to handle?

Would you rather be fully seen and risk rejection, or stay hidden to keep love?

We offer the following:

- PREMADE AND CUSTOM COVER
- PAPERBACK, HARDCOVER, DUSTJACKET
- FOILED (SPECIAL EDITION)
- SPRAYED EDGE
- PROMOTIONAL GRAPHICS
- AUDIOCOVERS

SURRENDER
TO THE
TIDES

Come to the depths, where the waters glow,
Where the currents whisper secrets below.
The sea will cradle you; the waves will kiss,
Come, dear sailor, and discover your bliss.
Drift with the tides; let the winds be still,
Follow my voice and surrender your will.
Beneath the moon, where shadows weave,
In the ocean's embrace, you'll never leave.

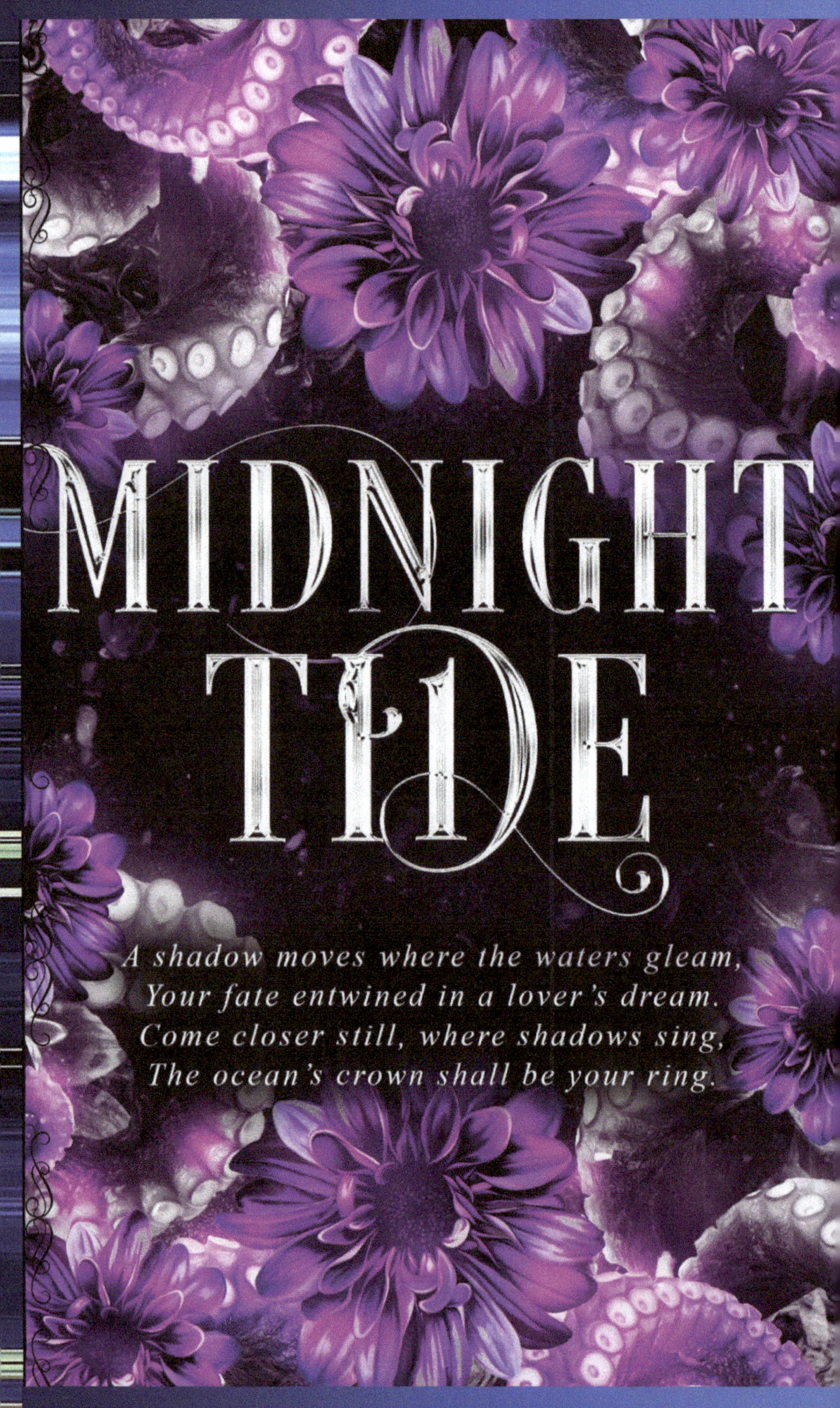

MIDNIGHT TIDE

A shadow moves where the waters gleam,
Your fate entwined in a lover's dream.
Come closer still, where shadows sing,
The ocean's crown shall be your ring.

DARK LURE
OF THE
SIREN

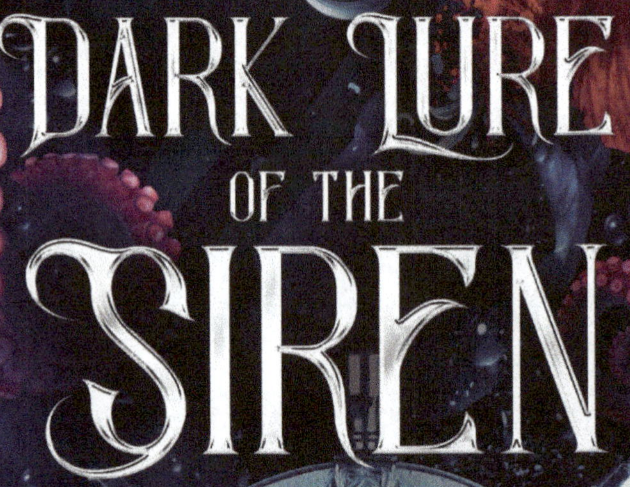

In shadowy depths where darkness creeps,
A chilling melody stirs from the deep.
With a voice like ice, sharp as a knife,
She summons the lost to dance with their life.

The waves crash and howl, a tempest's own song,
Her laughter, a taunt, where the damned belong.
"Come forth, you wanderers, your fate intertwined,
In my cold embrace, your freedom confined."

Her hair flows like darkness, entwined with despair,
With eyes like an abyss, the void's cruel glare.
Her kiss is the tempest, her touch the decay,
A promise of solace, a price you must pay.

As ships are drawn near, lit by ghostly flame,
The siren's dark whispers call out every name.
But lurking beneath that entrancing facade,
A hunger for souls, insatiable, flawed.

When the night falls silent, with souls claimed and spent,
The sea churns in fury, a malevolent bent.
Yet still on the currents, her haunting refrain,
A siren's sweet promise, a lover in pain.

So heed well, brave sailor, before you descend,
For her heart is the void, a chilling end.
In the depths of despair, where shadows entwine,
Lies beauty in darkness, a love most malign.

C.A. VARIAN
THE CURSED WATERS DUET

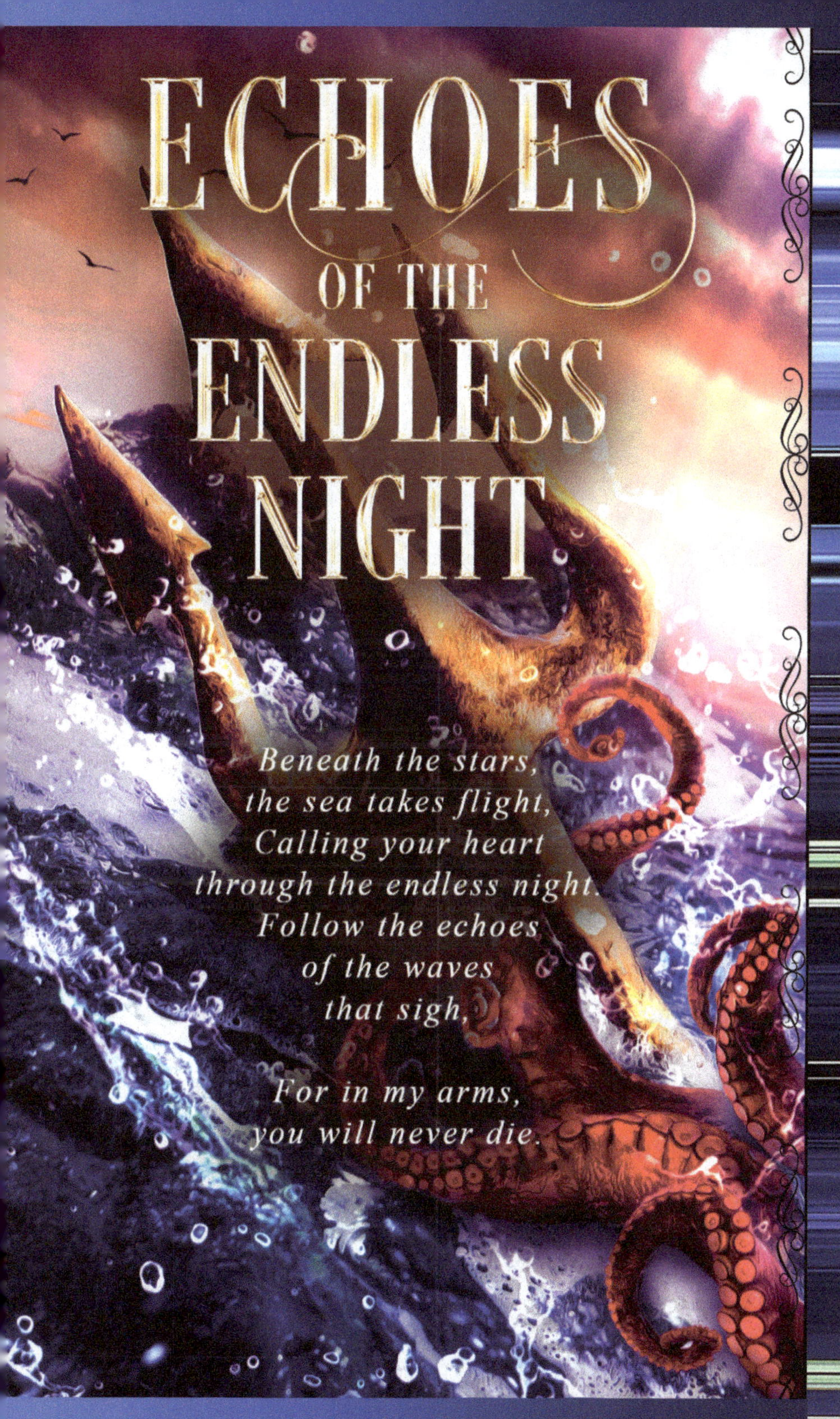

ECHOES
OF THE
ENDLESS
NIGHT

Beneath the stars,
the sea takes flight,
Calling your heart
through the endless night.
Follow the echoes
of the waves
that sigh,

For in my arms,
you will never die.

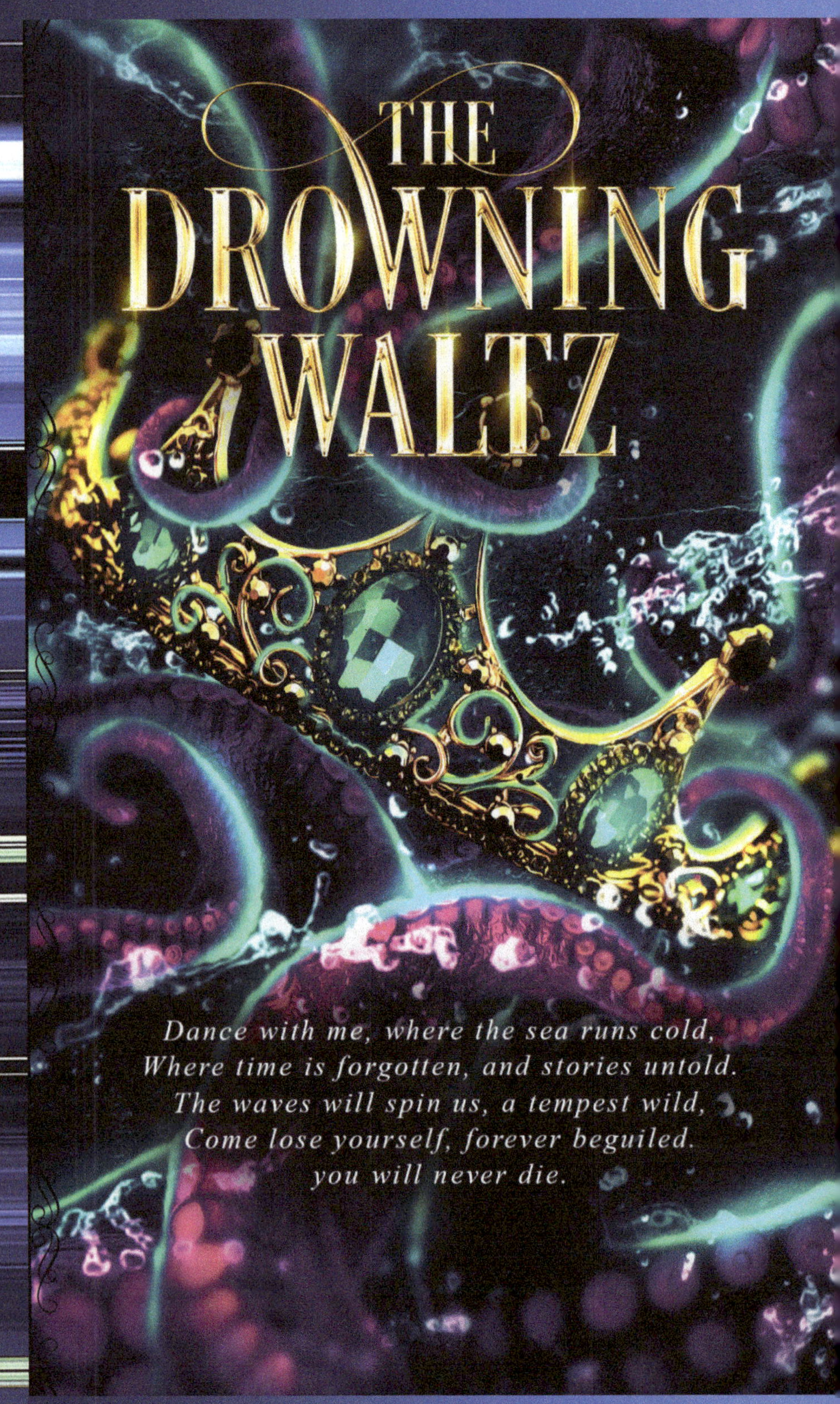

THE DROWNING WALTZ

Dance with me, where the sea runs cold,
Where time is forgotten, and stories untold.
The waves will spin us, a tempest wild,
Come lose yourself, forever beguiled.
you will never die.

THE OCEAN'S HAUNTING SERENADE

Come closer, love, where the sea meets the sky,
Where whispers linger, and sailors die.
The tide will pull, the waves will sing,
A haunting call, a fatal ring.
My hair like shadows, my lips like wine,
A treasure lost beneath the brine.
Your heartbeat thrums, a fleeting tune,
Beneath the gaze of the ghostly moon.
Surrender now, let the waters claim,
Your fleeting breath, your mortal name.
For in my arms, no pain shall stay,
Just timeless passion in the ocean's sway.
In the depths where dark memories thrive,
We'll dance through the currents, forever alive.
Embrace the enchantment, let the depths rise,
Together, we'll swim through stormy skies.

C. A. VARIAN

THE CURSED WATERS DUET

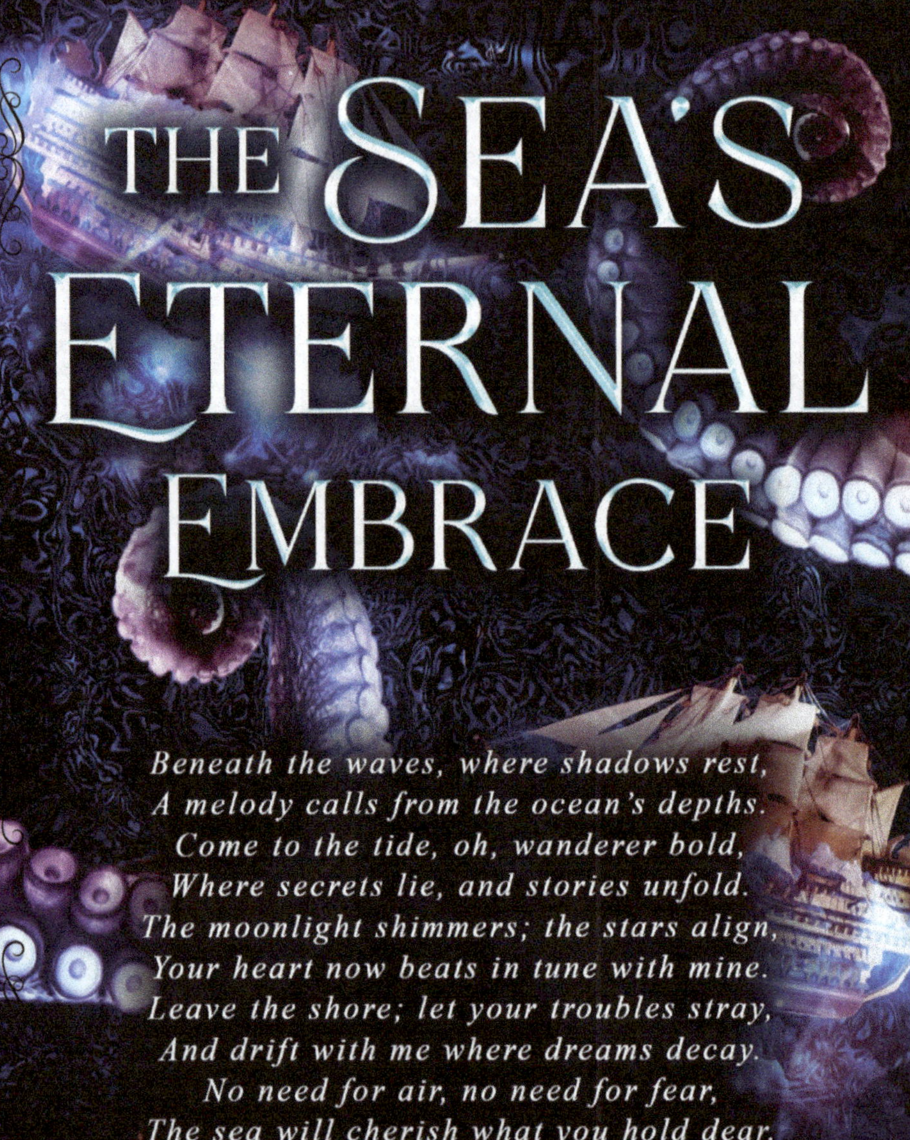

THE SEA'S ETERNAL EMBRACE

Beneath the waves, where shadows rest,
A melody calls from the ocean's depths.
Come to the tide, oh, wanderer bold,
Where secrets lie, and stories unfold.
The moonlight shimmers; the stars align,
Your heart now beats in tune with mine.
Leave the shore; let your troubles stray,
And drift with me where dreams decay.
No need for air, no need for fear,
The sea will cherish what you hold dear.
Come to the depths, oh sailor true,
For the ocean waits to cradle you.

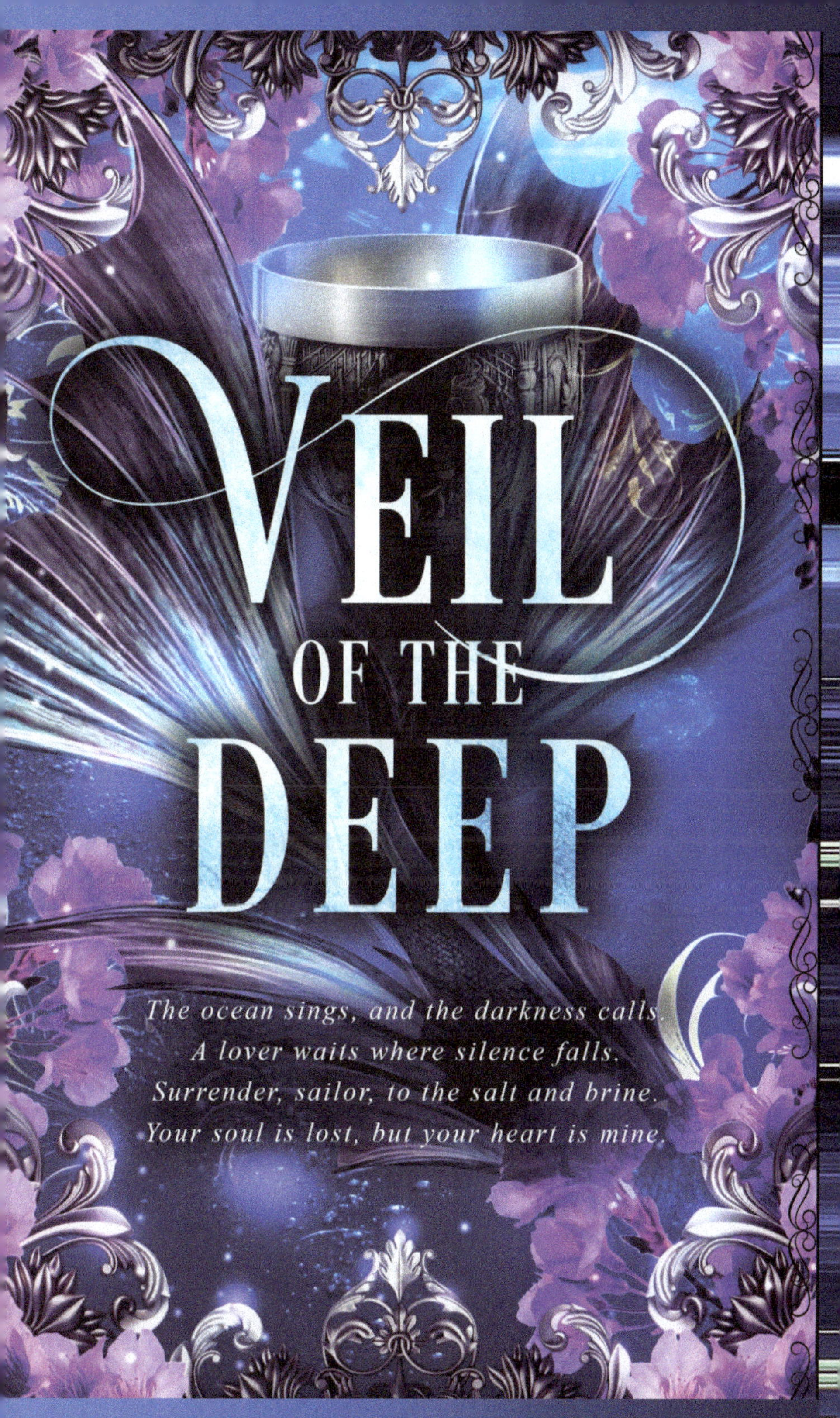

VEIL
OF THE
DEEP

The ocean sings, and the darkness calls.
A lover waits where silence falls.
Surrender, sailor, to the salt and brine.
Your soul is lost, but your heart is mine.

SIREN SECRETS

"He swore to return for you, but it has been centuries. Now, as the tide brings him back, you wonder—will you welcome him or make him pay?"

Describe your first words to him when he finally stands before you.

A Tide Between Worlds

MARKOS

The wind smelled of salt and wild thyme as we climbed the stone path toward the village of Starspell, our steps guided by the distant rise and fall of music and laughter. Light spilled across the sea in long, golden ribbons, stretching toward the cliffs as the sun slipped slowly out of sight. Below, lanterns flickered to life one by one, dotting the square with warmth. Somewhere among them, someone had begun to sing.

Ocevia walked beside me, barefoot, her stride unhurried but deliberate. Her back was straight, her chin high, and though her expression remained composed, there was a quiet certainty in her presence that hadn't existed before.

The last time we'd walked a path like this, she'd moved beneath a hood, wary of every shifting shadow, her voice barely louder than a breath. I could still see her in that alley behind the tavern—eyes wide, posture guarded—yet bold enough to point at me as if she were daring fate to answer. She'd been nervous and brave in the same breath, that contradiction so startling it had rendered me briefly speechless. I remembered the flush in her cheeks when I kissed her hand, the shy way she'd confessed she didn't know how to ride a horse, as if it might change the way I looked at her.

I hadn't known then what she was capable of becoming. Only that I wanted her to reach whatever future waited, and that I didn't want her to fall trying to get there.

Now, she moved with an assurance that no longer had to be declared. She was still quiet, still watchful, but rooted in a way that felt unshakable. The gown she wore shimmered in the fading light, a blend of sea-glass hues and moonlit silver, cinched at the waist with strands of gold and braided kelp. It looked as though the ocean had woven it for her. Regal, not because of a crown, but because of the way she wore it.

Not as a goddess. Not as a queen. Simply as herself.

As we crested the rise, the village unfurled beneath us—soft with lamplight and edged in sea mist, its rooftops scattered like shells along the shore. The tide pool clearing had been transformed for the wedding: driftwood benches arranged in gentle arcs, pale ribbons dancing from tall posts in the breeze, and sun-bleached shells strewn across the path like blessings cast in salt and bone.

Laughter rose from the crowd as children darted between guests, and someone strummed a lyre near the fire pit, weaving music into the warm dusk. And there, at the center of it all, stood Azure.

She turned as if drawn by a thread, her gaze landing on us, and her face lit instantly, a smile blooming wide and bright, so real it reached her eyes and hushed the world for a heartbeat.

There was no pause between recognition and motion.

Ocevia had taken barely another step before Azure was running toward her, arms open, her veil caught in the wind like a sail unfurling. When they collided, it was with the kind of embrace that stole the breath from your chest, full of tears and wind and a joy so deep it threatened to undo them both.

"You came," Azure whispered, her voice rough with emotion.

"Of course I did." Tears slipping from her eyes, Ocevia smiled. "I wouldn't miss this."

Azure leaned back just enough to study her face. "I wasn't sure if standing on land would still feel like a wound to you."

Ocevia's gaze didn't waver. "It used to," she said quietly. "Not anymore."

When they finally stepped apart, Elios stood waiting nearby. He said nothing at first, only reached out and clasped my forearm with the firm grip of someone who had bled beside me, who understood what it meant to return from places others hadn't.

"You look happy," he said. "*Whole.* I wasn't sure I'd see you again."

"Neither was I," I admitted, and gave him a half-smile that still felt strange on my face, but true.

He nodded once—the past acknowledged, but not invited in—then glanced toward the shore, where Azure stood beneath the driftwood arch. The sea whispered behind her, low and steady, as if reciting vows of its own.

There was no announcement. No fanfare. Just a quiet shift in the air, like the hush before something sacred. The ceremony began not with words, but with a look exchanged—two people, hands clasped, shadows long on the sand as the tide reached for them inch by inch.

"I would've found you in any world," Azure said, her voice breaking slightly.

Elios looked at her as if he could see the depths of the ocean in her eyes. "And I would've waited in every one until you did."

When he slipped the coral ring onto her finger, the crowd drew in a breath as one, their silence carrying something more than awe.

It wasn't celebration. It was recognition—like belief stirring again in the open air. As if none of them had truly expected love to survive what we'd endured, even if most would never know the full truth of it.

Beside me, Ocevia shifted her stance. Her shoulders lifted slightly, her chin tilted upward. She didn't smile, not outwardly, but I recognized the expression. Not sorrow. Reverence. And maybe, buried beneath it, the quiet the weight of memory.

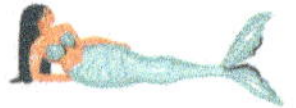

By the time we slipped away, the sky had deepened to a velvet blue, threaded with the last traces of sunset. Music floated up from the village in a slow, curling rhythm, laced with laughter and the clinking of glasses. But near the shore, the world felt quieter, holding only the silence of the sea and the distant echo of celebration.

Ocevia walked ahead of me, unhurried, her steps light in the tall grass. The wind tugged gently at the braids pinned along her head, loosening pale strands that traced along the curve of her spine. She looked as if she belonged to every part of this place, not only to the ocean that had shaped her, but to the cliffs, the sky, the darkening earth beneath our feet. There was nothing divided in her now.

At the edge of the sea, she paused, her gaze fixed on the horizon where waves met starlight. Her dress swept the grass with each shift of the breeze, the fabric catching glimmers of silver as she stood motionless.

She didn't speak right away, and I didn't fill the silence. There had always been a language between us that required no interruption, only presence.

When her voice came, it was soft, but certain. "The last time I stood in a village like this, I wore a stranger's cloak. I kept my eyes down and my hands closed. Every movement was borrowed. Every breath, survival."

I stayed beside her, listening to more than just her words and hearing the weight buried beneath them.

"I don't remember when I stopped hiding," she continued, almost to herself. "Maybe it wasn't one moment. Maybe it was a thousand small ones. But I stopped."

"I know."

She exhaled through her nose, the sound closer to a laugh. "It's strange. I thought I'd feel different. After ending Miris. After becoming what I am. People kneel when I pass now. Girls who once turned away from me whisper my name like a prayer." She turned to face me, her expression steady. "And I still feel like me. Just... clearer."

I met her gaze and, as always, was struck by the force of her stillness. "The first time I saw you," I said, "you were standing behind a tavern, wrapped in clothes that was too big for you like they were armor. You pointed at me."

Her cheeks colored, the faintest pink rising against the coolness of the evening air. "I regretted that for days. I thought I'd made a complete fool of myself."

"You didn't. I thought you were the bravest person I'd ever seen."

She laughed quietly then, not out of amusement, but from that space where vulnerability becomes something shared.

"You were terrified," I said gently.

"I was," she whispered. "But with you, I felt safe."

Her fingers found mine, threading with quiet purpose. "You didn't let me fall."

Lifting her hand to my lips, I brushed a kiss across her knuckles. The gesture echoed that first moment, but this time, her hand didn't tremble. It anchored me.

"You saved my life, Ocevia. Again and again."

"I didn't know what I was doing," she said. "When I brought you back, I was just trying to hold onto something that felt real."

"And that's what made it a miracle."

She leaned into me, her head resting against my shoulder, the curve of her body warm and familiar. The sea stretched out before us, singing in a softer key now, as though it rejoiced in our return.

My hand found the small of her back, fingers curling there without thought. Whether I was grounding her or myself, I didn't know.

"Do you ever miss who we were then?" I asked.

She was quiet for a moment, then said, "I miss the girl who got to fall in love with you for the first time, but I love the woman who gets to stay."

When she took my hand again, I knew it was not because she needed reassurance, but because she knew exactly where she wanted to be, and she wanted to be there with me. *Always.*

SIREN SECRETS

"A forbidden love between a mermaid and a mortal
—one doomed to dissolve into foam if discovered.
Yet, neither of you can stay away."

Describe your last night together before the sea
claims one of you forever.

REFLECTION

Have you ever loved
something you knew
you couldn't have?

What price would you
pay for love?

If you knew love was
temporary, would you
still choose it?

SIREN SECRETS

Describe the moment his hands reach for you. Are they gentle? Possessive? Both?

REFLECTION

Have you ever felt truly powerless?

Does desire thrive in captivity or in freedom?

If you could choose between escape and devotion, which would you take?

SIREN SECRETS

"He swore he loved you, but now you wonder—was he the hunter, or were you?"

Describe the moment you realize the truth.
Who really had the power all along?

REFLECTION

Have you ever been uncertain about someone's true intentions?

Is love ever truly without an agenda?

Have you ever felt like you were playing a game—only to realize you weren't the one in control?

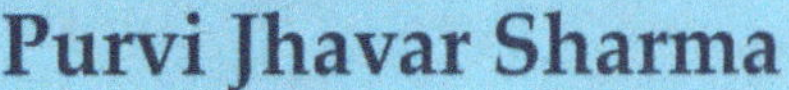

Purvi Jhavar Sharma

A published illustrator turning ideas into brilliant realities
with 8 years of experience in various types of artworks
such as graphic novels, children's books, sequential art
for comics, book covers and several other styles.
I would love to help you with your projects. Let's Connect!

www.dzign.in
jhawarpurvi@gmail.com

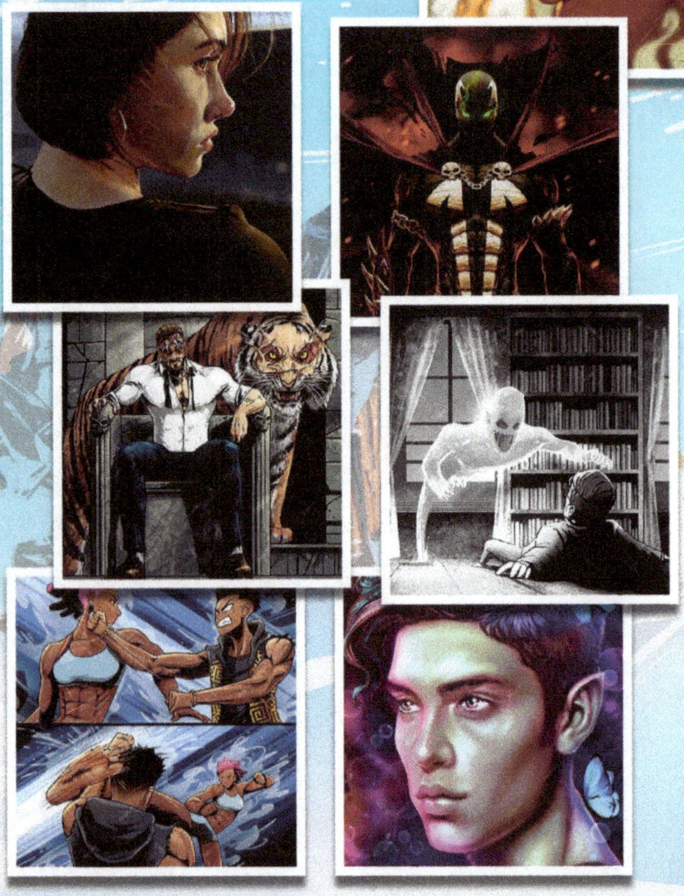

AZURE

SIREN SECRETS

"No matter how far you swim, something always pulls you back to him. Is it love, destiny, or a curse?"

Describe the moment you see him again after trying to escape. Do you run or stay?

JM DESIGNS
CUSTOM & PREMADE
COVER DESIGNS
ILLUSTRATED COVERS
JOLLYMEEK MALABAD
ArtistryMeek
bijorntolentino226@gmail.com
THE SEVENTH LORD
E. G. SPARKS
Throne FLAMES
AUTHOR NAME
Kingdom OF DECEIT And DESIRE
BOOK 1
MELINDA HAYDE
ILLUSTRATED ARTS

LUCENTHAVEN COVERS
AUTHOR NAME
THE OCEAN'S CHOSEN
VEIL OF SILVER WINE
LUCENTHAVEN COVERS
AUTHOR NAME
WICKED
LUCENTHAVEN COVERS
AUTHOR NAME
MOONBORN CHRONICLES
1
CALL OF THE MOON
"When darkness whispers, the moon answers"
LUCENTHAVEN COVERS
AUTHOR NAME
THE WINGBOUND SERIES BOOK 1
HOUSE OF WINGS
LUCENTHAVEN COVERS
AUTHOR NAME
THE GREED THAT RULES ALL
AUTHOR NAME
BROWSE OUR PORTFOLIO AND SERVICES!
lucenthavencovers.com

SIREN SECRETS

"Write about a dangerous romance where you saved someone you should have let go. Now, they won't stop chasing you."

Imagine saving a drowning man, only to realize he was never meant to survive. Now, he follows you— on land, in water, in dreams. Is he in love with you, or is he something else entirely?

Have you ever saved someone emotionally, only to regret it?

When has love felt more like a curse than a blessing?

What do you do when someone you once wanted becomes impossible to escape?

Pearl of the Sea

OCEVIA

Soft light filtered through the dome of the opalescent shell above, casting a glow like moonlight across the coral floor. Warmth lingered in the air, dry and still, a quiet heat untouched by the sea's usual pull. The room had been built not for current, but for breath. Sprigs of crushed sea rosemary hung in the corners, and salt-laced steam thickened the atmosphere. Beneath me, layers of silk and kelp-fiber sheets cradled my body, soothing the ache blooming low in my back.

I had shifted into my human form hours ago, long before the contractions began. The transformation felt natural and expected, as if my body had always known what was coming.

The sea was quiet beyond the walls, which only made my fear and anxiety worse. It was like the calm before the storm, and I knew the torrent was coming.

Although this was my first child, I was not afraid of the pain. I had endured pain. I had survived death, betrayal, war. But this was something different. Something I couldn't command. Something miraculous. For months, I had carried her beneath my heart—a child forged of hope, blood, and second chances. And now she was coming, and I could no longer protect her with my body alone.

Beside me, Markos sat with his hand wrapped tightly around mine. Without speaking, he pressed a cool cloth to my brow and brushed strands of damp hair from my cheek. When our eyes met, he smiled, but my worries were reflected in his expression too.

"You've survived monsters and miracles," he whispered. "But this... this is what makes you divine."

Even filled with worry, his voice steadied me more than any chant or charm ever could.

The next contraction built low and deep, spreading like fire through my hips. Clenching my teeth, I tightened my grip, feeling every inch of it. This was pain that carved and hollowed, yes, but also pain that brought forth a new life.

My midwife and dear friend, Elise, moved through the chamber, checking towels and vials, murmuring something to her apprentice before coming to my side. She was the calmest person in the room.

"Breathe, Your Grace."

Just as she said the words, my last contraction eased, and I sucked in a deep breath because I had to. Because my daughter needed me to.

Outside, the world waited.

But here, at this moment, I was not a goddess. Not a ruler. I was a woman, curled on a bed of silk, clinging to the hand of the man I loved, trying to be brave.

Time blurred. I didn't know how long I'd been lying there, knees drawn up, fingers locked around Markos's hand like letting go might break something essential. The contractions came like relentless crashing waves, splintering through my body and receding, only to return with greater force. I stopped counting. Lost in the rhythm, I focused only on surviving the storm rising in my blood.

Sweat soaked the hollow of my back, and my breath came in ragged gasps, causing the nausea to twist low in my belly. My legs shook without my permission and for a harrowing moment, I remembered what it felt like when the Kraken took me, when my body became something unrecognizable, unruly, terrifying. That same helpless surrender roared back through me now.

Only this time, I wasn't being overtaken by something monstrous.

This time, I was creating something beautiful.

Still, I hated how little control I had. I hated the feeling of splitting open, undone.

Tears stung my eyes as another contraction tore through me. "I can't—" I choked out, my tone desperate, although I knew no one could help me. "I can't do this."

Markos crouched until he was eye level with me, lifting my chin with his fingers until I couldn't look away from him. "You can, My Sea Maiden. You already are. Look at me."

Although I wanted to close my eyes and dream of being somewhere where the pain could not touch me, I did not see pity in his eyes, but belief. And gods help me, I clung to it.

He stayed at my side like a stone in a storm. Holding my hand through every surge. He whispered when my strength began to falter, his voice weaving through the pain like thread.

"You're doing this," he murmured again, his lips close to my ear. "I'm right here. You're not alone. I've got you."

Even when my grip turned to iron and my nails left crescent moons in his skin, he never pulled away. His eyes never left mine.

Across the room, Elise folded cloths with her apprentice by her side. Once the basin of water was filled, she finally knelt at the end of the bed, her gaze holding steady with mine. "It's time, Your Grace. Your little one is almost here."

The words echoed through me, but my body already knew. The pressure built, the burning stretch of bone and muscle undeniable, the primal urgency overwhelming.

A tremor rolled through me and I couldn't breathe. I couldn't speak, but Markos did, voice hoarse. Leaning close, he pressed his forehead to mine.

"She's almost here, my love. Just a little longer."

I didn't feel ready.

But I pushed.

Blinding pain consumed every part of me as I bore down, hoping my baby would be born healthy. Worrying that I wouldn't be enough for her. Every fear I'd ever had coming down to this one moment. All my insecurities.

Elise's voice pulled me out of my spiral, steadying me. "One more time."

I wasn't sure how I did it, but I pushed harder. The pressure peaked and held. One final, breathless second stretched long, and then split open.

A cry pierced the stillness, filling my heart in an instant.

The sound was high, fierce, gloriously alive.

Collapsing into the sheets, I gasped for air, every limb trembling and spent. I cried and laughed at once, unable to tell one from the other.

Through the blur, Elise turned with something small wrapped in sea-damp cloth. Her expression, always composed, softened.

"It's a beautiful baby girl."

Arms open, heart aching, I reached forward.

"Give her to me."

Taking my daughter into my arms was like nothing I had ever experienced or could ever imagine.

She was impossibly small. Limbs curled close, tiny fists trembling. Damp golden curls clung to her brow, the same soft hue as mine, and her skin was still flushed from the effort of being born. A hiccupping sound escaped her—not quite a cry and not yet a word.

Momentarily stunned, I blinked down at her with Markos leaning over my shoulder. She felt so light, so unfinished, like a thought still forming. I held her awkwardly at first, terrified I might drop her, or somehow break this fragile, wriggling thing I had just summoned from the deep.

Then she squirmed, let out a tiny mewl, and nestled against my chest with the sleepy certainty of someone who'd always belonged there.

My daughter.

Breath unsteady, Markos reached out and brushed his knuckles along her cheek. At his touch, something in his face cracked wide open. Awe bloomed there, unguarded and pure.

"She's perfect," he whispered, his voice catching on the last word. "Just like her mommy."

I looked down at her tiny features, from her trembling lip to the endless blue of her eyes, and felt my chest swell with a fullness too powerful to hold.

"I was so scared," I whispered. "I didn't feel strong enough. Not at the start. I didn't feel like a goddess. I didn't even feel like myself."

Lifting my hand, Markos pressed it to his lips. "You were more than strong enough. You brought her into the world. You gave her everything."

A shaky laugh escaped. "You mean I screamed her into existence."

He smiled. "You summoned her like a storm."

As though in answer to her daddy, Pearl hiccupped, but then promptly urinated on my chest.

I blinked, then laughed harder. "Oh. She's definitely mine."

Markos made a choked sound that might've been a laugh or a sob. "Fierce from the start."

Thumb moving slowly over mine, Markos anchored me in the quiet that followed. The room held stillness now, filled only with the soft rhythm of our daughter's breathing, the hush of water beyond the palace walls, the rustle of cloth as Elise finished her work.

We were safe. She was safe.

Once the bedding was clean, Elise stepped forward to check the baby's pulse, her temperature, the flush in her cheeks. With a small nod, she slipped away, leaving us in peace.

Leaning close, Markos spoke softly. "After all we've discussed, have you chosen a name?"

I looked down at her sleeping face, so small and perfect, and felt warmth rise in my chest like something settling into place.

"Pearl," I whispered. "That's her name."

He looked at her again, then back at me, a flicker of emotion tightening in his throat. "Why Pearl?"

I brushed a finger along her cheek, careful not to wake her. "Because pearls are made from wounds. Something sharp slips in and the body tries to protect itself. And from that pain, something beautiful grows."

Markos nodded, his eyes glassy. "It suits her."

Strong. Resilient. Quietly radiant.

Just like the girl who would bear it.

Also by C.A. Varian

Crown of the Phoenix Series

Crown of the Phoenix

Crown of the Exiled

Crown of the Prophecy

Mate of the Phoenix

Shadowed by Prophecy

Shadowed by the Veil (Coming Soon)

My Alien Mate Series

My Alien Protector

My Alien Rescuer (coming soon!)

Other World Series

The Other World

The Other Key

The Other Fate

Hazel Watson Mystery Series

Kindred Spirits: Prequel

The Sapphire Necklace

Justice for the Slain

Whispers from the Swamp

Crossroads of Death

The Spirit Collector

The Darkness that Follows (Coming 2025)

The Cursed Waters Duet

Song of Death

Goddess of Death

Survivor & Savior Duet

Saving Scarlett

Keeping Caroline

Standalones

Second Chance with Santa

When Everly Saved Emerald Hollow (Coming Soon
with A.A. Weaver)

Spirit of the Dying Flower (Coming Soon)

The Gladiatrix & the Fallen Son (Coming Soon)

Wings of the Forgotten (Coming Soon with J. Paige)

Born and raised in the heart of Louisiana's Cajun Country, I'm a passionate writer of dark, fantasy, paranormal, and even alien romances—if there's a romance involved, chances are I've written it. My stories are filled with mystery, magic, and intense emotional connections that keep readers on the edge of their seats.

When I'm not writing, you'll find me creating special editions of my books packed with all the bells and whistles—character art, exclusive swag, and more for my readers to treasure. I love connecting with fans, whether it's through my TikTok shop, my website, or in person at events where I can share the stories I pour my heart into.

A proud mother and new grandmother, I've faced many challenges in life, including a battle with chronic Lyme disease, but I've never let it define me. Writing is my escape and my passion, and with the support of my amazing assistant Jessica, my husband Trevor, and my daughters, Arianna and Brianna, I'm living my dream of writing full-time. Even my two youngest sisters pitch in, helping me with various tasks for the business—it's truly a family affair!

At home in Alabama, surrounded by love, laughter, and inspiration, I'm never without my two Shih Tzus, Charlie and Luna, along with my three mischievous cats—Ramses, Simba, and Cookie. Whether I'm doting on my furry companions, reading, or soaking up family time, every moment is a precious one.

Join me as I continue to create worlds full of romance, adventure, and unforgettable characters that you won't want to put down!

A VAULT OF ART & ECHOES
ARTIST & DESIGNER CREDITS

Main Cover Graphics by Geka
Hardcase Design D'Arte Oriel
Alternative Cover Design D'Arte Oriel
Edge Design Artwork D'Arte Oriel
Title Page Design Lucenthaven Covers
Scene Break Design Anastasy Helter
Activity Pages Design J. Paige (My amazing assistant, Jessica)

Artists Collections in order of appearance

D'Arte Oriel
Frina Art
Creative Valuation
Keni Aryani AKA Babelast
Cangxxx Graphics
Rosel Graphic Design
Creative Valuation
Izaac Brito
Wallflower Designs
Covers by Chan
ZONE ARTZ
Berberis Design
Covers & Berries
Cyan Book Cover Designs
Obsi Art
RJ Creatives
Athena Crest Arts
Lune Aesthete Designs
Xielle Covers
Graphics by Geka
SLM Creations
Creative Valuation
Swampy Sloth Studios
Leigh Graphic Design
Book Cover Trove
Achlys Book Cover Design
G-CAT Design Services

Various Artists & Designers

Prawney
Tatiana Mitrushova
Alvindo
Barv Art
Designer Candies
Alky
J Horrocks
Alky
Sergei Tokmakov
From the Everett Collection
Fernando Cortes
Susannp4
Designer Candies
Vika_Glitter

More Artist Collections

Artscandare
Creative Valuation
Purvi Jhavar Sharma
JM Designs
Lucenthaven Covers
NN Clipart

Coloring Page Designs ZONE ARTZ & J.Paige

Watercolor Illustrations by: b.illustrations, young generation team, bad designer, Liudmila Kopecka, Syifa Fauzia Zazuli, Anna Kuzmina, SPRESSO, Anna Szonn, Sontenn, Lordyswiss, Varvara Kurakina, Imgenes de gala ly, Creative Valuation, Anggiena Arifani, Oceanoart, Nichewatercolor, Elena Dorosh Art, johannes.k, deemakdaksina, Okinoma, Christana, Ronnie Morallos, and more via Canva.